Marion

The Story of an Artist's Model

Marion

The Story of an Artist's Model

Onoto Watanna

MINT EDITIONS

Marion: The Story of an Artist's Model was first published in 1916.

This edition published by Mint Editions 2021.

ISBN 9781513271569 | E-ISBN 9781513276564

Published by Mint Editions®

 MINT
EDITIONS

minteditionbooks.com

Publishing Director: Jennifer Newens
Design & Production: Rachel Lopez Metzger
Project Manager: Micaela Clark
Typesetting: Westchester Publishing Services

Contents

I

In dat familee dere are eleven cheeldren, and more—they come! See dat leetle one? She is très jolie! Oui, très jolie, n'est-ce pas? De father he come from Eengland about ten year ago. He was joost young man, mebbe twenty-seven or twenty-eight year ol', and he have one leetle foreign wife and six leetle cheeldren. They were all so cold. They were not use to dis climate of Canada. My wife and I, we keep de leetle 'otel at Hochelaga, and my wife she take all dose leetle ones and she warm dem before the beeg hall stove, and she make for dem the good French pea-soup."

Mama had sent me to the corner grocer to buy some things. Monsieur Thebeau, the grocer, was talking, and to a stranger. I felt ashamed and humiliated to hear our family thus discussed. Why should we always be pointed out in this way and made to feel conspicuous and freaky? It was horrid that the size of our family and my mother's nationality should be told to everyone by that corner grocer. I glared haughtily at Monsieur Thebeau, but he went garrulously on, regardless of my discomfiture.

"De eldest—a boy, monsieur—he was joost nine year old, and my wife she call him, 'Le petit père.' His mother she send him out to walk wiz all hees leetle sisters, and she say to him: 'Charles, you are one beeg boy, almost one man, and you must take care you leetle sisters; so, when de wind she blow too hard, you will walk you on de side of dat wind, and put yourself between it and your sisters.' 'Yes, mama,' il dit. And we, my wife and I, we look out de window, and me? I am laugh, and my wife, she cry—she have lost her only bebby, monsieur—to see dat leetle boy walk him in front of his leetle sisters, open hees coat, comme ça, monsieur, and spread it wiz hees hands, to make one shield to keep de wind from his sisters."

The man to whom Monsieur Thebeau had been speaking, had turned around, and was regarding me curiously. I felt abashed and angry under his compelling glance. Then he smiled, and nodding his head, he said:

"You are right. She *is* pretty—quite remarkably pretty!"

I forgot everything else. With my little light head and heart awhirl, I picked up my packages and ran out of the store. It was the first time I had been called pretty, and I was just twelve years old. I felt exhilarated and utterly charmed.

When I reached home, I deposited the groceries on a table in the kitchen and ran up to my room. Standing on a chair, I was able to see my face in the oval mirror that topped a very high and scratched old chiffonier. I gazed long and eagerly at the face I had often heard Monsieur Thebeau say was "très jolie," which French words I now learned must mean: "Pretty—quite remarkably pretty!" as had said that Englishman in the store.

Was I really pretty then? Surely the face reflected there was too fat and too red. My! my cheeks were as red as apples. I pushed back the offending fat with my two hands, and I opened my eyes wide and blinked them at myself in the glass. Oh! if only my hair were gold! I twisted and turned about, and then I made grimaces at my own face.

Suddenly I was thrilled with a great idea—one that for the moment routed my previous ambition to some day be an artist, as was my father. I would be an actress! If I were pretty, and both that Frenchman and Englishman had said so, why should I not be famous?

I slipped into mama's room, found a long skirt, and put it on me; also a feather which I stuck in my hair. Then, fearing detection, I ran out on tiptoe to the barn. There, marching up and down, I recited poems. I was pausing, to bow elaborately to the admiring audience, which, in my imagination, was cheering me with wild applause, when I heard mama's voice calling to me shrilly:

"Marion! Marion! Where in the world is that girl?"

"Coming, mama."

I divested myself hastily of skirt and feather, and left the barn on a run for the house. Here mama thrust our latest baby upon me, with instructions to keep him quiet while she got dinner. I took that baby in my arms, but I was still in that charmed world of dreams, and in my hand I clasped a French novel, which I had filched from my brother Charles' room. Charles at this time was twenty years of age, and engaged to be married to a girl we did not like.

I tried to read, but that baby would not keep still a minute. He wriggled about in my lap and reached a grimy hand after my book. Irritated and impatient, I shook him, jumped him up and down, and then, as he still persisted, I pinched him upon the leg. He simply yelled. Mama's voice screamed at me above the baby's:

"If you can't take better care of that baby, and keep him quiet, you shall not be allowed to paint with your father this afternoon, but shall sit right here and sew," a punishment that made me put down the book, and amuse the baby by letting him pull my hair, which seemed to make him supremely happy, to judge from his chuckles and shouts of delight.

ONOTO WATANNA

After dinner, which we had at noon, I received the cherished permission, and ran along to papa's room. Dear papa, whose gentle, sensitive hands are now at rest! I can see him sitting at his easel, with his blue eyes fixed absently upon the canvas before him. Papa, with the heart and soul of a great artist, "painting, painting," as he would say, with a grim smile, "pot-boilers to feed my hungry children."

I pulled out my paints and table, and began to work. From time to time I spoke to papa.

"Say, papa, what do I use for these pink roses?"

"Try rose madder, white and emerald green—a little naples yellow," answered papa patiently.

"Papa, what shall I use for the leaves?"

"Oh, try making your greens with blues and yellows."

From time to time I bothered him. By and by, I tired of the work, and getting up with a clatter, I went over and watched him. He was painting cool green waves dashing over jagged rocks, from a little sketch he had taken down at Lachine last summer.

"Tell me, papa," I said after a moment, "if I keep on learning, do you think I will ever be able to earn my living as an artist?"

"Who? What—you? Oh!" Absently papa blew the smoke about his head, gazed at me, but did not seem to see me. He seemed to be talking rather to himself, not bitterly, but just sadly:

"Better be a dressmaker or a plumber or a butcher or a policeman. There is no money in art!"

II

Next to our garden, separated only by a wooden fence, through which we children used to peep, was the opulent and well-kept garden of Monsieur Prefontaine, who was a very important man, once Mayor of Hochelaga, the French quarter of Montreal, in which we lived. Madame Prefontaine, moreover, was an object of unfailing interest and absorbing wonder to us children. She was an enormously fat woman, and had once taken a trip to New York City, to look for a wayward sister. There she had been offered a job as a fat woman for a big circus. Madame Prefontaine used to say to the neighbors, who always listened to her with great respect:

"Mon dieu! That New York—it is one beeg hell! Never do I feel so hot as in dat terrible city! I feel de grease it run all out of me! Mebbe, eef I stay at dat New York, I may be one beeg meelionaire—oui! But, non! Me? I prefer my leetle home, so cool and quiet in Hochelaga than be meelionaire in dat New York, dat is like purgatory."

We had an old straggly garden. Everything about it looked "seedy" and uncared for and wild, for we could not afford a gardener. My sisters and I found small consolation in papa's stout assertion that it looked picturesque, with its gnarled old apple trees and shrubs in their natural wild state. I was sensitive about that garden. It was awfully poor-looking in comparison with our neighbors' nicely kept places. It was just like our family, I sometimes treacherously thought—unkempt and wild and "heathenish." A neighbor once called us that. I stuck out my tongue at her when she said it. Being just next to the fine garden of Monsieur Prefontaine, it appeared the more ragged and beggarly, that garden of ours.

Mama would send us children to pick the maggots off the currant bushes and the bugs off the potato plants and, to encourage us, she would give us one cent for every pint of bugs or maggots we showed her. I hated the bugs and maggots, but it was fascinating to dig up the potatoes. To see the vegetables actually under the earth seemed almost like a miracle, and I would pretend the gnomes and fairies put them there, and hid inside the potatoes. I once told this to my little brothers and sisters, and Nora, who was just a little tot, wouldn't eat a potato again for weeks, for fear she might bite on a fairy. Most of all, I loved to pick strawberries, and it was a matter of real grief and humiliation to me that our own strawberries were so dried-up looking and small, as compared with the big, luscious berries I knew were in the garden of Monsieur Prefontaine.

On that day, I had been picking strawberries for some time, and the sun was hot and my basket only half full. I kept thinking of the berries in the garden adjoining, and the more I thought of them, the more I wished I had some of them.

It was very quiet in our garden. Not a sound was anywhere, except the breezes, making all kinds of mysterious whispers among the leaves. For some time, my eye had become fixed, fascinated, upon a loose board, with a hole in it near the ground. I looked and looked at that hole, and I thought to myself: "It is just about big enough for me to crawl through." Hardly had that thought occurred to me, when down on hands and knees I dropped, and into the garden of the great Monsieur Prefontaine I crawled.

The strawberry beds were right by the fence. Greedily I fell upon them. Oh, the exquisite joy of eating forbidden fruit! The fearful thrills that even as I ate ran up and down my spine, as I glanced about me on all sides. There was even a wicked feeling of fierce joy in acknowledging to myself that I was a thief.

"Thou shalt not steal!" I repeated the commandment that I had broken even while my mouth was full, and then, all of a sudden, I heard a voice, one that had inspired me always with feelings of respect and awe and fear.

"How you get in here?"

Monsieur Prefontaine was towering sternly above me. He was a big man, bearded, and with a face of preternatural importance and sternness.

I got up. My legs were shaky, and the world was whirling about me. I thought of the jail, where thieves were taken, and a great terror seized me. Monsieur Prefontaine had been the Mayor of Hochelaga. He could have me put in prison for all the rest of my life. We would all be disgraced.

"Well? Well? How you get in here?" demanded Monsieur Prefontaine.

"M'sieu, I—I-*crawled in*!" I stammered, indicating the hole in the fence.

"Bien! *Crawl out*, madame!"

"Madame" to me, who was but twelve years old!

"*Crawl out!*" commanded Monsieur, pointing to the hole, and feeling like a worm, ignominiously, under the awful eye of that ex-mayor of Hochelaga, on hands and knees and stomach, I crawled out.

Once on our side, I felt not the shame of being a thief so much as the degradation of *crawling out* with that man looking.

Feeling like a desperate criminal, I swaggered up to the house, swinging my half-filled basket of strawberries. As I came up the path, Ellen, a sister just two years older than I, put her head out of an upper window and called down to me:

"Marion, there's a beggar boy coming in at the gate. Give him some of that stale bread mama left on the kitchen table to make a pudding with."

The boy was about thirteen, and he was a very dirty boy, with hardly any clothes on him. As I looked at him, I was thrilled with a most beautiful inspiration. I could regenerate myself by doing an act of lovely charity.

"Wait a minute, boy."

Disregarding the stale bread, I cut a big slice of fresh, sweet-smelling bread that Sung Sung, our one very old Chinese servant, had made that day. Heaping it thick with brown sugar, I handed it to the boy.

"There, beggar boy," I said generously, "you can eat it all."

He took it with both hands, greedily, and now as I looked at him another, a fiendish, impulse seized me. Big boys had often hit me, and although I had always fought back as valiantly and savagely as my puny fists would let me, I had always been worsted, and had been made to realize the weakness of my sex and age. Now as I looked at that beggar boy, I realized that here was my chance to hit a big boy. He was smiling at me gratefully across that slice of sugared bread, and I leaned over and suddenly pinched him hard on each of his cheeks. His eyes bulged with amazement, and I still remember his expression of surprise and pained fear. I made a horrible grimace at him and then ran out of the room.

III

There was a long, bleak period, when we knew acutely the meaning of what papa wearily termed "Hard Times." Even in "Good Times" there are few people who buy paintings, and no one wants them in Hard Times.

Then descended upon Montreal a veritable plague. A terrible epidemic of smallpox broke out in the city. The French and not the English Canadians were the ones chiefly afflicted, and my father set this down to the fact that the French Canadians resisted vaccination. In fact, there were anti-vaccination riots all over the French quarter, where we lived.

And now my father, in this desperate crisis, proved the truth of the old adage that "Blood will tell." Ours was the only house on our block, or for that matter the surrounding blocks, where the hideous, yellow sign, "PICOTTE" (smallpox), was not conspicuously nailed upon the front door, and this despite the fact that we were a large family of children. Papa hung sheets all over the house, completely saturated with disinfectants. Every one of us children was vaccinated, and we were not allowed to leave the premises. Papa himself went upon all the messages, even doing the marketing.

He was not "absent-minded" in those days, nor in the grueling days of dire poverty that followed the plague. Child as I was, I vividly recall the terrors of that period, going to bed hungry, my mother crying in the night and my father walking up and down, up and down. Sometimes it seemed to me as if papa walked up and down all night long.

My brother Charles, who had been for some time our main support, had married (the girl we did not like) and although he had fervently promised to continue to contribute to the family's support, his wife took precious care that the contribution should be of the smallest, and she kept my brother, as much as she could, from coming to see us.

A day came when, with my mother and it seemed all of my brothers and sisters, I stood on a wharf waving to papa on a great ship. There he stood, by the railing, looking so young and good. Papa was going to England to try to induce grandpa—that grandfather we had never seen—to help us. We clung about mama's skirts, poor little mama, who was half distraught and we all kept waving to papa, with our hats and hands and handkerchiefs and calling out:

"Good-bye, papa! Come back! Come back soon!" until the boat was only a dim, shadowy outline.

The dreadful thought came to me that perhaps we would never see papa again! Suppose his people, who were rich and grand, should induce our father never to return to us!

I had kept back my tears. Mama had told us that none of us must let papa see us cry, as it might "unman" him, and she herself had heroically set the example of restraining her grief until after his departure. Now, however, the strain was loosened. I fancied I read in my brothers' and sisters' faces—we were all imaginative and sensitive and excitable—my own fears. Simultaneously we all began to cry.

Never will I forget that return home, all of us children crying and sobbing, and mama now weeping as unconcealedly as any of us, and the French people stopping us on the way to console or commiserate with us; but although they repeated over and over:

"Pauvre petites enfants! Pauvre petite mère!" I saw their significant glances, and I knew that in their minds was the same treacherous thought of my father.

But papa did return! He could have stayed in England, and, as my sister Ada extravagantly put it, "lived in the lap of luxury," but he came back to his noisy, ragged little "heathens," and the "painting, painting of pot-boilers to feed my hungry children."

IV

"M onsieur de St. Vidal is ringing the doorbell," called Ellen, "why don't you open the door, Marion? I believe he has a birthday present for you in his hand."

It was my sixteenth birthday, and Monsieur de St. Vidal was my first beau! He was a relative of our neighbors, the Prefontaines, and I liked him pretty well. I think I chiefly liked to be taken about in his stylish little dogcart. I felt sure all the other girls envied me.

"You go, Ellen, while I change my dress."

I was anxious to appear at my best before St. Vidal. It was very exciting, this having a beau. I would have enjoyed it much more, however, but for the interfering inquisitiveness of my sisters, Ada and Ellen, who never failed to ask me each time I had been out with him, whether he had "proposed" yet or not.

Ellen was running up the stairs, and now she burst into our room excitedly, with a package in her hand.

"Look, Marion! Here's your present. He wouldn't stop—just left it, and he said, with such a Frenchy bow—whew! I don't like the French!— 'Pour Mamselle Marion, avec mes compliments!'" and Ellen mimicked St. Vidal's best French manner and voice.

I opened the package. Oh, such a lovely box of paints—a perfect treasure!

"Just exactly what I wanted!" I cried excitedly, looking at the little tubes, all shiny and clean, and the new brushes and palette.

Ada was sitting reading by the window, and now she looked up and said:

"Oh, did that French *wine merchant* give that to Marion?"

She cast a disparaging glance at the box, and then, addressing Ellen, she continued:

"Marion is disgustingly old for sixteen, but, of course, if he gives her *presents*" (he had never given me anything but candy before) "he will propose to her, I suppose. Mama married at sixteen, and I suppose *some* people—" Ada gave me another look that was anything but approving—"*are* in a hurry to get married. *I* shall never marry till I am twenty-five!" Ada was twenty.

This time, Ellen, who was eighteen, got the condemning look. Ellen was engaged to be married to an American editor, who wrote to her every day in the week and sometimes telegraphed. They were awfully in love with each other. Ellen said now:

"Oh, he'll propose all right. Wallace came around a whole lot, you know, before he actually popped."

"Well, maybe so," said Ada, "but I think we ought to know that French wine merchant's intentions pretty soon. I'll ask him if you like," she volunteered.

"No, no, don't you dare!" I protested.

"Well," said Ada, "if he doesn't propose to you soon, you ought to stop going out with him. It's bad form."

I *wished* my sisters wouldn't interfere in my affairs. They nagged me everlastingly about St. Vidal, and it made me conscious when I was with him. They acted like self-appointed monitors. The minute I would get in, they would begin:

"Well, did he propose?" and I would feel ashamed to be obliged to admit, each time, that he had not. Ada had even made some suggestions of how I might "bring him to the point." She said men had to be led along like sheep. Ellen, however, had warmly vetoed those suggestions, declaring stoutly that Wallace, her sweetheart, had needed no prodding. In fact, he had most eloquently and urgently pleaded his own suit, without Ellen "putting out a finger" to help him, so she said.

That evening St. Vidal called and took me to the rink, and I enjoyed myself hugely. He was a graceful skater, and so was I, and I felt sure that everyone's eye was upon us. I was very proud of my "beau," and I secretly wished that he was blond. I did prefer the English type. However, conscious of what was expected of me by my sisters, I smiled my sweetest on St. Vidal, and by the time we started for home, I realized, with a thrill of anticipation, that he was in an especially tender mood. He helped me along the street carefully and gallantly.

It was a clear, frosty night, and the snow was piled up as high as our heads on each side of the sidewalks. Suddenly St. Vidal stopped, and drawing my hand through his arm, he began, with his walking stick, to write upon the snow:

"Madame Marion de St. Vida—"

Before he got to the "l," I was seized with panic. I jerked my hand from his arm, took to my heels and ran all the way home.

Now it had come—that proposal, and I did not want it. It filled me with embarrassment and fright. When I got home, I burst into Ada's room, and gasped:

"It's done! He did propose! B-but I said—I said—" I hadn't said anything at all.

"Well?" demanded Ada.

"Why, I'm not going to, that's all," I said.

Ada returned to the plaiting of her hair. Then she said sceptically:

"Hm, that's very queer. Are you *sure* he proposed, because *I* heard he was all the time engaged to a girl in Côte des Neiges."

"Oh, Ada," I cried, "do you suppose he's a bigamist? I think I'm fortunate to have escaped from his snare!"

The next day Madame Prefontaine told mama that St. Vidal had said he couldn't imagine what in the world I had run away suddenly from him like that for, and he said:

"Maybe she had a stomach ache."

V

E llen, don't you wish something would happen?"

Ellen and I were walking up and down the street near the English church.

"Life is so very dull and monotonous," I went on. "My! I would be glad if something real bad happened—some sort of tragedy. Even that is better than this deadness."

Ellen looked at me, and seemed to hesitate.

"Yes, it's awful to be so poor as we are," she answered, "but what I would like is not so much money as fame, and, of course, love. That usually goes with fame."

Ellen's fiancé was going to be famous some day. He was in New York, and had written a wonderful play. As soon as it was accepted, he and Ellen were to be married.

"Well, I tell you what I'd like above everything else on earth," said I sweepingly. "I would love to be a great actress, and break everybody's heart. It must be perfectly thrilling to be notorious, and we certainly are miserable girls!"

We were chewing away with great relish the contents of a bag of candy.

"Anyhow," said Ellen, "you seem to be enjoying that candy," and we both giggled.

Two men were coming out of the side door of the church. Attracted by our laughter, they came over directly to us. One of them we knew well. He was Jimmy McAlpin, the son of a fine old Scotch, very rich, lady, who had always taken an especial interest in our family. Jimmy, though he took up the collection in church, had been, so I heard the neighbors whisper to mama, once very dissipated. He had known us since we were little girls, and always teased us a lot. He would come up behind me on the street and pull my long plait of hair, saying:

"Oh, pull the string, gentlemen and ladies, and the figure moves!"

Now he came smilingly up to us, followed by his friend, a big, stout man, with a military carriage and gray mustache. I recognized him, too, though we did not know him. He was a very rich and important citizen of our Montreal. Of him also I had heard bad things. People said he was "fast." That was a word they always whispered in Montreal, and shook their heads over, but whenever I heard it, its very mystery and badness

ONOTO WATANNA

somehow thrilled me. Ada said there was a depraved and low streak in me, and I guiltily admitted to myself that she was right.

"What are you girls laughing about?" asked Jimmy, a question that merely brought forth a fresh accession of giggles.

Colonel Stevens was staring at me, and he had thrust into his right eye a shining monocle. I thought him very grand and distinguished-looking, much superior to St. Vidal. Anyway we were tired of the French, having them on all sides of us, and, as I have said, I admired the blond type of men. Colonel Stevens was not exactly blond, for his hair was gray (he was bald on top, though his hat covered that), but he was typically British, and somehow the Englishmen always appeared to me much superior to our little French Canucks, as we called them.

Said the Colonel, pulling at his mustache:

"A laughing young girl in a pink cotton frock is the sweetest thing on earth."

I had on a pink cotton frock, and I was laughing. I thought of what I had heard Madame Prefontaine say to mama—in a whisper:

"He is one dangerous man—dat Colonel Steven, and any woman seen wiz him will lose her reputation."

"Will I lose mine?" I asked myself. I must say my heart beat, fascinated with the idea.

Something now was really happening, and I was excited and delighted.

"Can't we take the ladies—" I nudged Ellen—"some place for a little refreshment," said the Colonel.

"No," said Ellen, "mama expects us home."

"Too bad," murmured the Colonel, very much disappointed, "but how about some other night? To-morrow, shall we say?" Looking at me, he added: "May I send you some roses, just the color of your cheeks?"

I nodded from behind Ellen's back.

"Come on," said Ellen brusquely, "we'd better be getting home. You know you've got the dishes to do, Marion."

She drew me along. I couldn't resist looking back, and there was that fascinating Colonel, standing stock-still in the street, still pulling at his mustache, and staring after me. He smiled all over, when I turned, and blew me an odd little kiss, like a kind of salute, only from his lips.

That night, when Ellen and I were getting ready for bed, I said:

"Isn't the Colonel thrillingly handsome though?"

"Ugh! I should say not," said Ellen. "Besides he's a married man, and a flirt."

"Well, I guess he doesn't love his old wife," said I.

"If she is old," said Ellen, "so is he—maybe older. Disgusting."

All next day I waited for that box of roses, and late in the afternoon, sure enough, it came, and with it a note:

DEAR MISS MARION

Will you and your charming sister take a little drive with me and a friend this evening? If so, meet us at eight o'clock, corner of St. James and St. Denis streets. My friend has seen your sister in Judge Laflamme's office" (Ellen worked there) "and he is very anxious to know her. As for me, I am thinking only of when I shall see my lovely rose again. I am counting the hours!

Devotedly,
FRED STEVENS

The letter was written on the stationery of the fashionable St. James Club. Now I was positive that Colonel Stevens had fallen in love with me. I thought of his suffering because he could not marry me. In many of the French novels I had read men ran away from their wives, and, I thought: "Maybe the Colonel will want me to elope with him, and if I won't, perhaps, he will kill himself," and I began to feel very sorry to think of such a fine-looking soldierly man as Colonel Stevens killing himself just because of me.

When I showed Ellen the letter, after she got home from work, to my surprise and delight, she said:

"All right, let's go. A little ride will refresh us, and I've had a hard week of it, but better not let mama know where we're going. We'll slip out after supper, when she's getting the babies to sleep."

Reaching the corner of St. James and St. Denis Streets that evening, we saw a beautiful closed carriage, with a coat of arms on the door, and a coachman in livery jumped down and opened the door for us. We stepped in. With the Colonel was a middle-aged man, with a dry, yellowish face and a very black—it looked dyed—mustache.

"Mr. Mercier," said the Colonel, introducing us.

"Oh," exclaimed Ellen, "are you the Premier?"

"Non, non, non," laughed Mr. Mercier, and turning about in the seat, he began to look at Ellen and to smile at her, until the ends of his waxed

ONOTO WATANNA

mustache seemed to jump up and scratch his nose. Colonel Stevens had put his arm just at the back of me, and as it slipped down from the carriage seat to my waist, I sat forward on the edge of the seat. I didn't want to hurt his feelings by telling him to take his arm down, and still I didn't want him to put it around me. Suddenly Ellen said:

"Marion, let's get out of this carriage. That beast there put his arm around me, and he pinched me, too." She indicated Mercier.

She was standing up in the carriage, clutching at the strap, and she began to tap upon the window, to attract the attention of the coachman. Mr. Mercier was cursing softly in French.

"Petite folle!" he said, "I am not meaning to hurt you—joost a little loving. Dat is all."

"You ugly old man," said Ellen, "do you think I want *you* to love me? Let me get out!"

"Oh, now, Miss Ellen," said the Colonel, "that is too rude. Mr. Mercier is a gentleman. See how sweet and loving your little sister is."

"No, no," I cried, "I am not sweet and loving. He had no business to touch my sister."

Mr. Mercier turned to the Colonel.

"For these children did you ask me to waste my time?" and putting his head out of the carriage, he simply roared:

"Rue Saint Denis! Sacré!"

They set us down at the corner of our street. When we got in a friend of papa's was singing to mama and Ada in the parlor:

> "In the gloaming, oh, my darling,
> When the lights are dim and low."

He was one of many Englishmen, younger sons of aristocrats, who, not much good in England, were often sent to Canada. They liked to hang around papa, whose family most of them knew. This young man was a thin, harmless sort of fellow, soft-spoken and rather silly, Ellen and I thought; but he could play and sing in a pretty, sentimental way and mama and Ada would listen by the hour to him. He liked Ada, but Ada pretended she had only an indifferent interest in him. His father was the Earl of Albemarle, and Ellen and I used to make Ada furious by calling her "Countess," and bowing mockingly before her.

Walking on tiptoe, Ellen and I slipped by the parlor door, and up to our own room. That night, after we were in bed, I said to Ellen:

"You know, I think Colonel Stevens is in love with me. Maybe he will want me to elope with him. Would you if you were me?"

"Don't be silly. Go to sleep," was Ellen's cross response. She regretted very much taking that ride, and she said she only did it because she got so tired at the office all day, and thought a little ride would be nice. She had no idea, she said, that those "two old fools" would act like that.

I was not going to let Ellen go to sleep so easily, however.

"Listen to this," I said, poking her to keep her awake. "This is Ella Wheeler Wilcox, Ellen, and they call her the Poet of Passion." Ellen groaned, but she had to listen:

> *"Just for one kiss that thy lips had given*
> *Just for one hour of bliss with thee,*
> *I would gladly barter my hopes of heaven,*
> *And forfeit the joys of eternity;*
> *For I know in the way that sins are reckoned*
> *That this is a sin of the deepest dye,*
> *But I also know if an angel beckoned,*
> *Looking down from his home on high,*
> *And you adown by the gates Infernal*
> *Should lift to me your loving smile,*
> *I would turn my back on the things Eternal,*
> *Just to lie on your breast awhile."*

"Ugh!" said Ellen, "I would scorn to lie on Colonel Stevens' old fat breast."

VI

Wallace, Ellen's sweetheart, had not sold his play, but he expected to any day. He was, however, impatient to be married—they had now been engaged over a year—and he wrote Ellen that he could not wait, anyway more than two or three months longer. Meanwhile Ellen secured a better position.

The new position was at a much greater distance from our house, and as she had to be at the office early, she decided to take a room farther down town. Papa at first did not want her to leave home, but Ellen pointed out that Hochelaga was too far away from her office, and then she added, to my delight, that she'd take me along with her. I could make her trousseau and cook for us both, and it wouldn't cost any more for two than for one.

Mama thought we were old enough to take care of ourselves. "For," said she, "when I was Ellen's age I was married and had two children. Besides," she added, "we are crowded for room, in the house, and it will only be for a month or two."

So Ellen secured a little room down town. I thought the house was very grand, for there was thick carpet on all the floors and plush furniture in the parlor.

We were unpacking our trunk, soon after we arrived, when there was a knock at our door, and in came Mrs. Cohen, our landlady and a big fat man. Mrs. Cohen pointed at us with a pudgy finger:

"There they are!" she explained. "Ain't they smart? Look at that one," pointing to Ellen, "she is smart like a lawyer, and the sister," pointing to me, "she is come to work and sew like she was the wife, see."

She turned about then and yelled at the top of her voice:

"Sarah! Sarah! Where is that lazy Sarah? Come! Directly!"

A young, thin girl with a clear skin and enormous black eyes came slowly up the stairs and into the room.

"See, Sarah," cried Mrs. Cohen, "there is two girls that is more smart than you. That one, she is just the same age as you, and she makes good money, yes. She makes twelve dollar a week. *You* cannot do that. Oh, no!"

Sarah looked at us sullenly, and to our greeting: "How do you do?" she returned: "How's yourself?" Then turning savagely on her father and stepmother, she snarled:

"And if I can't make money, whose fault is it? I have to work more hard than a servant even, with all those children of yours!"

"Sarah, Sarah! be more careful of your speech!" cried her mother. "Did not the God above give to you those six little brothers? You should thank Him for His kindness."

She started down the stairs, followed by her husband. Sarah, however, stayed in the room, and now she smiled at us in a friendly way.

"Say, Miss—What's your names?"

"Ellen and Marion."

"Well, say, my stepmother is the limit. Gosh! I wish we were not Jews. Nobody likes us."

"You ought not to say that," said Ellen, severely, "the Jews were God's chosen people, remember."

"Gosh!" said Sarah, "I wish He didn't choose me."

That evening, Sarah thrust her face in at our door, and called in a loud whisper:

"Say, girls, do youse want to see two old fools? Come on then."

She led us, all tiptoeing, into a room next to one occupied by a little English old maid named Miss Dick, who gave music lessons for twenty-five cents a lesson, and who always spoke in a sort of hissing whisper, so that a little spit came from her lips. Mrs. Cohen called it the "watering can."

"Kneel down there," said Sarah, pointing to a crack in the wall. I peeped through, and this is what I saw: Seated in the armchair was a funny little old man—I think he was German—with a dried, wrinkled face. Perched on the arm of the chair was Miss Dick. They were billing and cooing like turtle doves, and she was saying:

"Am I your little Dicky-birdie?" and he was looking proud and pleased.

Ellen and I burst into fits of laughter, but Sarah pulled us away, and we covered our mouths and stifled back the laughter. When we got to our room, Sarah told us that the old man, Schneider, had come to her father and mother and asked them to find him a wife. Her mother agreed to do so for the payment of ten dollars. She had spoken to Miss Dick, and the latter had also agreed to pay ten dollars.

About a week after we had been there, Miss Dick and Mr. Schneider were married. They had packed up all Miss Dick's things and were going down the stairs with bags in their hands, when Mrs. Cohen ran out into the hall.

ONOTO WATANNA

"Now please, like a lady and gentleman, pay me the ten dollars each as we made the bargain, for I make you acquainted to get married."

"Ten dollars!" screamed Miss Dick.

"Yes, you make the bargain with me."

"I made no such bargain," cried the bride shrilly. "We met and loved at first sight." Turning to Schneider, who was twirling his thumbs, she said: "Protect me, dearie."

He said:

"I say nutting. I say nutting."

"*Will* you pay that debt?" demanded Mrs. Cohen and then, as Miss Dick did not answer, she pointed dramatically to my sister Ellen, who was standing with me laughing at the head of the stairs. "You see that lady. She is just the same as a lawyer, and she say you should pay. Pay for your man like a lady, that smart lady up there say you should."

"Oh, oh! you old Shylock!" screamed Miss Dick hissingly. Mrs. Cohen was obliged to wipe her face and, backing away, she cried:

"Don't you Shylock me with your watering can."

Ellen and I were doubled up with laughter, and Mrs. Cohen seized hold of a broom, and literally swept bride and groom from the house, shouting at them all sorts of epithets and curses.

VII

We had been at Cohen's less than a month, when Wallace wrote he could wait no longer.

He had not sold his play, but he had a very good position now as associate editor of a big magazine, and he said he was making ample money to support a wife. So he was coming for his little Ellen at once. We were terribly excited, particularly as Wallace followed up the letter with a telegram to expect him next day, and sure enough the next day he arrived.

He did not want any "fussy" wedding. Only papa and I were to be present. Wallace did not even want us, but Ellen insisted. She looked sweet in her little dress (I had made it), and although I knew Wallace was good and a genius and adored my sister, I felt broken-hearted at the thought of losing her, and it was all I could do to keep from crying at the ceremony.

As the train pulled out, I felt so utterly desolate that I stretched out my arms to it and cried out aloud:

"Ellen, Ellen, please don't go. Take me, too."

I never realized till then how much I loved my sister. Dear little Ellen, with her love of all that was best in life, her sense of humor, her large, generous heart, and her absolute purity. If only she had stayed by my side I am sure her influence would have kept me from all the mistakes and troubles that followed in my life, if only by her disgust and contempt of all that was dishonorable and unclean. But Wallace had taken our Ellen, and I had lost my best friend, my sister and my chum.

That night I cried myself to sleep. I thought of all the days Ellen and I played together. Even as little girls mama had given us our special house tasks together. We would peel potatoes and shell peas or sew together, and as we worked we would tell each other stories, which we invented as we went along. Our stories were long and continuous, and full of the most extravagant and unheard of adventures and impossible riches, heavenly beauty and bravery that was wildly reckless.

There was one story Ellen continued for weeks. She called it: "The Princess who used Diamonds as Pebbles and made bonfires out of one-hundred-dollar bills." I made up one called: "The Queen who Tamed Lions and Tigers with a Smile," and more of that kind.

Mama would send Ellen and me upon messages sometimes quite a distance from our house, for we had English friends living at the other side of the town. The French quarter was cheaper to live in and that was why we lived in Hochelaga. Ellen and I used to walk sometimes three miles each way to Mrs. McAlpin's house on Sherbrooke Street. To vary the long walk we would hop along in turn, holding one another's legs by the foot, or we would walk backward, counting the cracks in the sidewalks that we stepped over. One day a young man stood still in the street to watch us curiously. Ellen was holding one of my feet and I was hopping along on the other. He came up to us and said:

"Say, sissy, did you hurt your foot?"

"No," I returned, "we're just playing Lame Duck."

It was strange now, as I lay awake, crying over the going of my sister, that all the queer little funny incidents of our childhood together came thronging to my mind. I vividly remembered a day when mama was sick and the doctor said she could have chicken broth. Well, there was no one home to kill the chicken, for that was the time papa went to England. Ellen and I volunteered to kill one, for Sung Sung, our old servant, believed it would be unlucky to kill one with the master away—one of his everlasting superstitions. Ellen and I caught the chicken. Then I held it down on the block of wood, while Ellen was to chop the head off. Ellen raised the hatchet, but when it descended she lowered it very gently, and began to cut the head off slowly. Terrified, I let go. Ellen was trembling, and the chicken ran from us with its head bleeding and half off.

"Qu'est-ce que c'est? Qu'est-ce que c'est? De little girl, she is afraid. See me, I am not scared of nutting."

It was the French grocer boy. He took that unfortunate chicken, and placing its bleeding head between the door and jamb, he slammed the door quickly, and the head was broken. I never did like that boy, now I hated him. Ellen looked very serious and white. When we were plucking the feathers off later, she said:

"Marion, do you know we are as guilty as Emile and if it were a human being, we could be held as accomplices."

"No, no, Ellen," I insisted. "I did not kill it. I am not guilty. I wouldn't be a murderer like Emile for anything in the world."

"You're just as bad," said Ellen severely, "perhaps worse, because to-night you'll probably eat part of your victim."

I shuddered at the thought, and I did not eat any chicken that night.

When I was packing my things, preparatory to leaving Mrs. Cohen's next morning, for I was to return home, now that Ellen was married, Mrs. Cohen came in with a large piece of cake in her hand. She was very sorry for me because I had lost my sister.

"There," she said, "that will make you feel better. Taste it. It is good." I could not eat their cake, because she used goose grease instead of butter, but I didn't want to hurt her feelings and I pretended to take a bite. When she was not looking I stuffed it into the wastepaper basket.

"Now never mind about your sister no more," she said kindly. "The sun will shine in your window some day."

I was still sniffing and crying, and I said:

"It looks as if it were going to rain to-day."

"Vell then," she said, "it vill not be dry."

VIII

I was at an age—nearly eighteen now—when girls want and need chums and confidantes. I was bubbling over with impulses that needed an outlet, and only foolish young things like myself were capable of understanding me. With Ellen gone, I sought and found girl friends I believed to be congenial.

My sister Ada, because of her superiority in age and character to me, would not condescend to chum with me. Nevertheless, she heartily disapproved of my choice in friends, and constantly reiterated that my tastes were low. Life was a serious matter to Ada, who had enormous ambitions, and had already been promised a position on our chief newspaper, to which she had contributed poems and stories. To Ada, I was a frivolous, silly young thing, who needed constantly to be squelched, and she undertook to do the squelching, unsparingly, herself.

"Since we are obliged," said Ada, "to live in a neighborhood with people who are not our equals, I think it a good plan to keep to ourselves. That's the only way to be exclusive. Now, that Gertie Martin" (Gertie was my latest friend) "is a noisy American girl. She talks through her nose, and is always criticizing the Canadians and comparing them with the Yankees. As for that Lu Fraser" (another of my friends) "she can't even speak the Queen's English properly, and her uncle keeps a saloon."

Though I stoutly defended my friends, Ada's nagging had an unconscious effect upon me, and for a time I saw very little of the girls.

Then one evening, Gertie met me on the street, and told me that, through her influence, Mr. Davis (also an American) had decided to ask me to take a part in "Ten Nights in a Bar Room," which was to be given at a "Pop" by the Montreal Amateur Theatrical Club, of which he was the head. I was so excited and happy about this that I seized hold of Gertie and danced with her on the sidewalk, much to the disgust of my brother Charles, who was passing with his new wife.

Mr. Davis taught elocution and dramatic art, and he was a man of tremendous importance in my eyes. He was always getting up concerts and entertainments, and no amateur affair in Montreal seemed right without his efficient aid. The series of "Pops" he was now giving were patronized by all the best people of the city and he had an imposing list of patrons and patronesses. Moreover the plays were to be produced in a real theatre, not merely a hall, and so they had somewhat the character of professional performances.

To my supreme joy, I was given the part of the drunkard's wife, and there were two glorious weeks in which we rehearsed and Mr. Davis trained us. He said one day that I was the "best actress" of them all, and he added that although he charged twenty-five dollars a month to his regular pupils he would teach me for ten, and if I couldn't afford that, for five, and if there was no five to be had, then for nothing. I declared fervently that I would repay him some day, and he laughed, and said: "I'll remind you when that 'some day' comes."

Well, the night arrived, and I was simply delirious with joy. I learned how to "make up," and I actually experienced stage fright when I first went on, but I soon forgot myself.

When I was crawling on the floor across the stage, trying to get something to my drunken husband, a voice from the audience called out:

"Oh, Mar-ri-on! Oh, Ma-ri-on! You're on the bum! You're on the bum!"

It was my little brother Randle, who, with several small boys had got free seats away up in front, by telling the ticket man that his sister was playing the star part. I vowed mentally to box his ears good and hard when I got home.

When the show was over, Mr. Davis came to the dressing room, and said, right before all the girls:

"Marion, come to my studio next week, and we'll start those lessons, and when we put on the next 'Pop,' which I believe will be 'Uncle Tom's Cabin,' we will find a good part for you."

"Oh, Mr. Davis," I cried, "are you going to make an actress of me?"

"We'll see! We'll see!" he said, smiling. "It will depend on yourself, and if you are willing to study."

"I'll sit up all night long and study," I assured him.

"The worst thing you could do," he answered. "We want to save these peaches," and he pinched my cheek.

Mr. Davis did lots of things that in other men would have been offensive. He always treated the girls as if they were children. People in Montreal thought him "sissified," but I am glad there are some men more like the gentler sex.

So I began to take lessons in elocution, and dramatic art. Oh! but I was a happy girl in those days. It is true, Mr. Davis was very strict, and he would make me go over lines again and again before he was satisfied, but when I got them finally right and to suit him, he would rub his hands, blow his nose and say:

"Fine! Fine! There's the real stuff in you."

He once said that I was the only pupil he had who had an atom of promise in her. He declared Montreal peculiarly lacking in talent of that sort, though he said he had searched all over the place for even a "spark of fire." I, at least, loved the work, was deadly in earnest and, finally, so he said, I was pretty, and that was something.

We studied "Camille," "The Marble Heart" and "Romeo and Juliet." All of my spare time at home, I spent memorizing and rehearsing. I would get a younger sister, Nora, who was absorbedly interested, to act as a dummy. I would make her be Armand or Armand's father.

"Now, Nora," I would say, "when I come to the word 'Her,' you must say: 'Camille! Camille'!"

Then I would begin, addressing Nora as Armand:

"You are not speaking to a cherished daughter of society, but a woman of the world, friendless and fearless. Loved by those whose vanity she gratifies, despised by those who ought to pity her—her—*Her*—"

I would look at Nora and repeat: "Her—!" and Nora would wake up from her trance of admiration of me and say:

"Camel! Camel!"

"No, no!" I would yell, "*That* is—" (pointing to the right—Mr. Davis called that "Dramatic action") "*your* way! *This* way—" (pointing to the left) "is mine!"

Then throwing myself on the dining-room sofa, I would sob and moan and cough (Camille had consumption, you may recall), and what with Nora crying with sympathy and excitement, and the baby generally waking up, there would be an awful noise in our house.

I remember papa coming half-way down the stairs one day and calling out:

"What in the devil is the matter with that Marion? Has she taken leave of her senses?"

Mama answered from the kitchen:

"No, papa, she's learning elocution and dramatic art from Mr. Davis; but I'm sure she's not suited to be an actress, for she lisps and her nose is too short. But do make her stop, or the neighbors will think we are quarreling."

"Stop this minute!" ordered papa, "and don't let me hear any more such nonsense."

I betook myself to the barn.

IX

The snow was crisp and the air as cold as ice. We were playing the last performance of "Uncle Tom's Cabin." We had been playing it for two weeks, and I had been given two different parts, Marie Claire, in which, to my joy, I wore a gold wig and a lace tea-gown—which I made from an old pair of lace curtains and a lavender silk dress mama had had when they were rich and she dressed for dinner—and Cassy. I did love that part where Cassy says:

"Simon Legree, you are afraid of me, and you have reason to be, for I have got the devil in me!"

I used to hiss those words at him and glare until the audience clapped me for that. Ada saw me play Cassy one night, and she went home and told mama that I had "sworn like a common woman before all the people on the stage" and that I ought not to be allowed to disgrace the family. But little I cared for Ada in those days. *I* was learning to be an actress!

On this last night, in fact, I experienced all the sensations of a successful star. Someone had passed up to me, over the footlights if you please, a real bouquet of flowers, and with these clasped to my breast, I had retired smiling and bowing from the stage.

To add to my bliss, Patty Chase, the girl who played Topsy, came running in to say that a gentleman friend of hers was "crazy" to meet me. He was the one who had sent me the flowers. He wanted to know if I wouldn't take supper with him and a friend and Patty that night.

My! I felt like a regular professional actress. To think an unknown man had admired me from the front, and was actually seeking my acquaintance! I hesitated, however, because Patty was not the sort of girl I was accustomed to go out with. I liked Patty pretty well myself, but my brother Charles had one day come to the house especially to tell papa some things about her—he had seen me walking with Patty on the street—and papa had forbidden me to go out with her again. As I hesitated, she said:

"It isn't as if they are strangers, you know. One of them, Harry Bond, is my own fellow. You know who his folks are, and but for them we'd have been married long ago. Well, Harry's friend, the one who wants to meet you, is a swell, too, and he hasn't been out from England long. Harry says his folks are big nobs over there, and he is studying law here.

His folks send him a remittance and I guess it's a pretty big one, for he's living at the Windsor, and I guess he can treat us fine. So come along. You'll not get such a chance again."

"Patty," I said, "I'm afraid I dare not. Mama hates me to be out late, and, see, it's eleven already."

"Why, the night's just beginning," cried Patty.

There was a rap at the door, and Patty exclaimed:

"Here they are now!"

All the girls in the room were watching me—enviously, I thought—and one of them made a catty remark about Patty, who had gone out in the hall, and was whispering to the men. I decided not to go, but when I came out of the room there they were all waiting for me and Patty exclaimed:

"Here she is," and, dragging me along by the hand, she introduced me to the men.

I found myself looking up into the face of a tall young man of about twenty-three. He had light curly hair and blue eyes. His features were fine and clear-cut, and, to my girlish eyes, he appeared extraordinarily handsome and distinguished, far more so even than Colonel Stevens, who had, up till then, been my ideal of manly perfection. Everything he wore had an elegance about it from his evening suit and the rich fur-lined overcoat to his opera hat and gold-topped cane. I felt flattered and overwhelmingly impressed to think that such a fine personage should have singled me out for especial attention. What is more, he was looking at me with frank and undisguised admiration. Instead of letting go my hand, which he had taken when Patty introduced us, he held it while he asked me if he couldn't have the pleasure of taking me out to supper. As I hesitated, blushing and awfully thrilled by the hand pressing mine, Patty said:

"She's scared. Her mother won't let her stay out late at night. She's never been out to supper before."

Then she and Harry Bond burst out laughing, as if that were a good joke on me, but Mr. Bertie (his name was the Honorable Reginald Bertie—pronounced Bartie) did not laugh. On the contrary, he looked very sympathetic, and pressed my hand the closer. I thought to myself:

"My! I must have looked lovely as Marie St. Claire. Wait till he sees me as Camille."

"I'm not afraid," I contradicted Patty, "but mama will be worried. She sits up for me."

This was not strictly true, but it sounded better than to say that Ada was the one who always sat up for anyone in the house who went out at night. She even used to sit up for my brother Charles before he was married, and I could just imagine the cross-questioning she would put me through when I got in late. Irritated as I used to be in those days at what I called Ada's interference in my affairs, I know now that she always had my best good at heart. Poor little delicate Ada! with her passionate devotion and loyalty to the family and her fierce, antagonistic attitude to all outside intrusion. She was morbidly sensitive.

Mr. Bertie quieted my fears by dispatching a messenger boy to our house with a note saying that I had gone with a party of friends to see the Ice Palace.

Even with Ada in the back of my mind, I was now, as Patty would say, "out for a good time," and when Mr. Bertie carefully tucked the fur robes of the sleigh about me, I felt warm, excited and recklessly happy.

We drove over to the Square, where the Ice Palace was erected. The Windsor Hotel was filled with American guests who were on the balconies watching the torchlight procession marching around the mountain. My brother Charles was one of the snow-shoers, and the men were all dressed in white and striped blanket overcoats with pointed capuchons (cowls) on their backs or heads, and moccasins on their feet.

It was a beautiful sight, that procession, and looked like a snake of light, winding about old Mount Royal, and when the fireworks burst all about the monumental Ice Palace, inside of which people were dancing and singing, really it seemed to me like a scene in fairyland. I felt a sense of pride in our Montreal, and looking up at Mr. Bertie, to note the effect of so much beauty upon him, I found him watching me instead.

The English, when they first come out to Canada, always assume an air of patronage toward the "Colonials," as they call us, just as if, while interested, they are also highly amused by our crudeness. Now Mr. Bertie said:

"We've seen enough of this Ice Palace's hard, cold beauty. Suppose we go somewhere and get something warm inside us. Gad, I'm dry."

Harry told the driver to take us to a place whose name I could not catch, and presently we drew up before a brilliantly lighted restaurant. Harry Bond jumped out, and Patty after him. I was about to follow when I felt a detaining hand upon my arm, and Bertie called out to Bond:

"I've changed my mind, Bond. I'll be hanged if I care to take Miss Ascough into that place."

Bond was angry, and demanded to know why Bertie had told him to order supper for four. He said he had called the place up from the theatre. I thought that queer. How could they have known I would go, since I had not decided till the last minute?

"Never mind," said Bertie. "I'll fix it up with you later. Go on in without us. It's all right."

Harry and Patty laughed, and, arm-in-arm, they went into the restaurant. All the time Bertie had kept a hand on my arm. I was too surprised and disappointed to utter a word, and after he had again tucked the rug about me, he said gently:

"I wouldn't take a sweet little girl like you into such a place, and that Patty isn't a fit person for you to associate with."

I said:

"You must think I'm awfully good."

I was disappointed and hungry.

"Yes, I do think so," he said gravely.

"Well, I'm not," I declared. "Besides, I'm going to be an actress, and actresses can do lots of things other people get shocked about. Mr. Davis says they are privileged to be unconventional."

"You, an actress!" he exclaimed. He said the word as if it were something disgraceful, like Ada might have said it.

"Yes," I returned. "I'll die if I can't be one."

"Whatever put such an idea in your head. You're just a refined, innocent, sweet, adorable little girl, far too sweet and pure and lovely to live such a dirty life."

He was leaning over me in the sleigh, and holding my hand under the fur robe. I thought to myself: "Neither St. Vidal nor Colonel Stevens would make love as thrillingly as he can, and he's certainly the handsomest person I've ever seen."

I felt his arm going about my waist, and his young face come close to mine. I knew he was going to kiss me, and I had never been kissed before. I became agitated and frightened. I twisted around and pulled away from him so that despite his efforts to reach my lips his mouth grazed, instead, my ear. Much as I really liked it, I said with as much hauteur as I could command:

"Sir, you have no right to do that. How dare you?"

He drew back, and replied coldly:

"I beg your pardon, I'm sure. I did not mean to offend you."

He hadn't offended me at all, and I was debating how on earth I was to let him know he hadn't, and at the same time keep him at the "proper distance" as Ada would say, when we stopped in front of our house. He helped me out, and lifting his hat loftily, was bidding me good-bye when I said shyly:

"M-Mr. Bertie, you—you d-didn't offend me."

Instantly he moved up to me and eagerly seized my hand. His face looked radiant, and I did think him the most beautiful man I had ever seen. With a boyish chuckle, he said:

"I'm coming to see you to-morrow night. May I?"

I nodded, and then I said:

"You mustn't mind our house. We're awfully poor people." I wanted to prepare him. He laughed boyishly at that and said:

"Good heavens, that's nothing. So are most of my folks—poor as church mice. As far as that goes, I'm jolly poor myself. Haven't a red cent except what the governor sends out to me. I'm going to see *you* anyway, and not your house."

He looked back at the driver whose head was all muffled up under his fur collar. Then he said:

"Will you give me that kiss now?"

I returned faintly:

"I c-can't. I think Ada's watching from the window."

He looked up quickly.

"Who's Ada?"

"My sister. She watches me like a hawk."

"Don't blame her," he said softly, and then all of a sudden he asked:

"Do you believe in love at first sight?"

"Yes," I answered. "Do you?"

"Well, I didn't—till to-night, but, by George, I do—now!"

X

I am not likely to forget that first call of Reginald Bertie upon me. I had thought about nothing else, and, in fact, had been preparing all day.

I fixed over my best dress and curled my hair. I cleaned all of the lower floor of our house, and dusted the parlor and polished up the few bits of furniture, and tried to cover up the worn chairs and horsehair sofa.

Every one of the children had promised to "be good," and I had bribed them all to keep out of sight.

Nevertheless, when the front doorbell rang that evening, to my horror, I heard the wild, noisy scampering of my two little brothers down the stairs, racing to see which should be the first to open the door; and trotting out from the dining-room right into the hall came Kathleen, aged three, and Violet, four and a half. They had been eating bread and molasses and had smeared it all over their faces and clothes, and they stood staring solemnly at Mr. Bertie as though they had never seen a man before. On the landing above, looking over the banister, and whispering and giggling, were Daisy, Lottie and Nellie.

Oh, how ashamed I felt that he should see all those dirty, noisy children. He stood there by the door, staring about him, with a look of amazement and amusement on his face; and, as he paused, the baby crawled in on hands and knees. She had a meat bone in her hand, and she squatted right down at his feet, and while staring up at him, wide-eyed, she went right on loudly sucking on that awful bone.

My face was burning, and I felt that I never could live down our family. Suddenly he burst out laughing. It was a boyish, infectious laugh, which was quickly caught up and mocked and echoed by those fiendish little brothers of mine.

"Are there any more?" he demanded gaily. "My word! They are like little steps and stairs."

I said:

"How do you do, Mr. Bertie?"

He gave me a quizzical glance, and said in a low voice:

"What's the matter with calling me 'Reggie?'"

Nora had run down the stairs and now, to my intense relief, I could hear her coaxing the children to come away, and she would tell them a story. Nora was a wonderful story-teller, and the children would listen to her by the hour. So would all the neighbors' children. I had told her that if she kept the children out of sight I would give her a piece of ribbon on which she had set her heart. So she was keeping her word, and presently I had the satisfaction of watching her go off with the baby on one arm, Kathleen and Violet holding to her other hand and skirt, and the boys in the rear.

Mr. Bertie, or "Reggie," as he said I was to call him, followed me into the "parlor." It was a room we seldom used in winter on account of the cold, but I had coaxed dear papa to help me clean out the fireplace—the only way it was heated—our Canadian houses did not have furnaces in those days—and the boys had brought me in some wood from the shed. So, at least, we had a cheerful fire crackling away in the grate, and although our furniture was old, it did not look so bad. Besides he didn't seem to notice anything except me, for as soon as we got inside he seized my hands and said:

"Give you my word, I've been thinking about you ever since last night."

Then he pulled me up toward him, and said:

"I'm going to get that kiss to-night."

Just then in came mama and Ada, and feeling awfully embarrassed and confused, I had to introduce him. Mama only stayed a moment, but Ada settled down with her crochet work by the lamp. She never worked in the parlor on other nights, but she sat there all of that evening, with her eye on Mr. Bertie and occasionally saying something brief and sarcastic. Mama said, as she was going out:

"I'll send papa right down to see Mr. Bertie. He looks so much like papa's brother who died in India. Besides, papa always likes to meet anyone from home."

Papa came in later, and he and Mr. Bertie found much to talk about. They had lived in the same places in England, and even found they knew some mutual friends and relatives. Papa's sisters were all famous sportswomen and hunters. One was the amateur tennis champion, and, of course, Mr. Bertie had heard of her.

Then papa inquired what he was doing in Montreal, and Bertie said he was studying law, and hoped to pass his finals in about eight months.

Then, he added that as soon as he could get together a fair practice, he expected to marry and settle down in Montreal. When he said that, he looked directly at me, and I blushed foolishly, and Ada coughed significantly and sceptically.

I really didn't get a chance to talk to him all evening, and even when he was going I could hardly say good-bye to him for mama came back with Daisy and Nellie, the two girls next to me, and what with Ada and papa there besides and everybody wishing him good-bye and mama inviting him to call again, I found myself almost in the background. He smiled, however, at me over mama's head, and he said, while shaking hands with her:

"I'll be delighted. May I come—er—to-morrow night?"

I saw Ada glance at mama, and I knew what was in their minds. Were they to be forced to go through this all again? The dressing up, the suppressing of the children, the using of the unused parlor, the burning of our fuel in the fireplace, etc. Papa, however, said warmly:

"By all means. I've some pretty good sketches of Macclesfield I'd like to show you."

"That will be charming," said my caller and, with a smile and bow that included us all, he was gone.

I did not get that kiss after all, and I may as well confess I was disappointed.

XI

The winter was passing into spring and Reggie had been a regular visitor at our house every night. The family had become used, or as Ada put it "resigned," to him. Though she regarded him with suspicion and thought papa ought to ask his "intentions," she knew that I was deeply in love with him. She had wrung this admission from me and she expressed herself as being sorry for me.

Because of Reggie's dislike for everything connected with the stage, I had stopped my elocution lessons and I was making some money at my painting. We had had a fine carnival that winter, and I did a lot of work for an art store, painting snow scenes and sports on diminutive toboggans, as souvenirs of Canada. These American visitors bought and I had, for a time, all the work I could do. This work and, of course, Reggie's strenuous objections kept my mind from my former infatuation.

Then, one night, he took me to see Julia Marlowe in "Romeo and Juliet." All my old passion and desire to act swept over me, and I nearly wept to think of having to give it up. When we were going home, I told Reggie how I felt, and this is what he said:

"Marion, which would you prefer to be, an actress or my wife?"

We had come to a standstill in the street. Everything was quiet and still, and the balmy sweetness of the Spring night seemed to enwrap even this ugly quarter of the city in a certain charm and beauty. I felt a sweet thrilling sense of deep tenderness and yearning toward Reggie, and also a feeling of gratitude and humility. It seemed to me that he was stooping down from a very great height to poor, insignificant me. More than ever he seemed a wonderful and beautiful hero in my young eyes.

"Well, dear?" he prompted, and I answered with a soft question:

"Reggie, do you really love me?"

"My word, darling," was his reply. "I fell in love with you that first night."

"But perhaps that was because I—I looked so nice as Marie Claire," I suggested tremulously. I wanted to be, oh, so sure of Reggie.

"You little goose," he laughed. "It was because you were you. Give me that kiss now. It's been a long time coming."

I had known him three months, but not till that night had we had an opportunity for "that kiss," and it *was* sweet, and I the very happiest girl in the world.

"Now we must hurry home," said Reggie, "as I want to speak to your father, as that's the proper thing to do, you know."

"Let's not tell papa yet," I said. "I *hate* the proper thing, Reggie. Why do you always want to be 'proper.'"

Reggie looked at me, surprised.

"Why, dear girl, it's the proper thing to be—er—proper, don't you know."

There was something so stolidly English about Reggie and his reply. It made me laugh, and I slipped my hand through his arm and we went happily down the street. Just for fun—I always liked to shock Reggie, he took everything so seriously—I said:

"Don't be too cocksure I'll marry you. I still would love to be an actress."

"My word, Marion," said he. "Whatever put such a notion in your head? I wish you'd forget all about the rotten stage. Actresses are an immoral lot."

"Can't one be immoral without being an actress?" I asked meekly.

"We won't discuss that," said Reggie, a bit testily. "Let's drop the dirty subject."

When he was going that night, and after he had kissed me good-bye several times in the dark hall, he said—but as if speaking to himself:

"Gad! but the governor's going to be purple over this."

The "governor" was his father.

XII

"The summer days are coming
The blossoms deck the bough,
The bees are gaily humming
And the birds are singing now."

I was singing and thumping on our old cracked piano. Ada said:
"For heaven's sakes, Marion, stop that noise, and listen to this advertisement."

I had been looking in the papers for some time in the hope of getting some permanent work to do. I was not making much money at my fancy painting, and papa's business was very bad. Ada was working on the "Star," and was helping the family considerably. She was the most unselfish of girls, and used to bring everything she earned to mama. She fretted all the time about the family and especially mama, to whom she was devoted. Poor little soul, it did seem as if she carried the whole weight of our troubles on her little shoulders.

I had been engaged to Reggie now a year. He had failed in his law examinations, and that meant another year of waiting, for, as he said, it would be impossible to marry until he passed. He had decided to go to England this summer, to see if the "governor" wouldn't "cough up" some more cash, and he said he would then tell his family about our engagement. He had not told them that yet. He had expected to after passing his examinations, but having failed in these, he had to put it off, he explained to me.

Ada used to say of Reggie that he was a "monument of selfishness and egotism," and that he spent more on himself for his clothes and expensive rooms and other luxuries than papa did on our whole family. She repeatedly declared that he was quite able to support a wife, and that his only reason for putting off our marriage was because he hated to give up any of the luxuries to which he was accustomed. In fact, Ada had taken a dislike to my Reggie, and she even declared that St. Vidal against whom she had been merely prejudiced because he was a French wine-merchant, would have been more desirable.

Anyway, Ada insisted that it was about time for me to do something toward the support of our family. Here I was nineteen years old and scarcely earning enough to pay for my own board and clothes.

"Read that."

She handed me the "Star," and pointed to the advertisement:

WANTED: A young lady who has talent to work for an artist. Apply to Count von Hatzfeldt, Château de Ramezay, rue Notre Dame.

"Why," I exclaimed, "that must be the old seigniory near the Notre Dame Cathedral."

"Of course, it is," said Ada. "I was reading in the papers that they are going to make it into a museum of historical and antique things. It used to be the home of the first Canadian governors, and there are big cannons down in the cellars that they used. If I were you, I'd go right over there now and get that work. There won't be many applicants, for only a few girls can paint."

I was as eager as Ada, and immediately set out for the Château de Ramezay.

It was a long ride, for we only had horse-cars in those days, and the Château was on the other end of the city. I liked the ride, however, and looked out of the window all of the way. We passed through the most interesting and historical part of our city, and when we came to the dismal, mottled, old stone jail, I could not help shuddering as I looked up at it, and recalled what my brother Charles used to tell me about it when I was a little girl. He said it was mottled because the house had small-pox. If we did this or that, we would be thrown into that small-pox jail and given black bread and mice to eat, and when we came out we would be horribly pock-marked. He said all the anti-vaccination rioters had been locked up in there, and they were pitted with marks.

As my car went by it, I could see the poor prisoners looking out of the barred windows and a great feeling of fear and pity for the sorrows of the world swept over me, so that my eyes became blinded with tears. A covered van was going in at the gate. A woman next to me said:

"There's the Black Maria. Look! There's a young girl in it!"

My heart went out to that young girl, and I wondered vaguely what she could have done that would make them shut her up in that loathsome "pock-marked" jail.

When we reached the French hospital, "Hôtel Bon Dieu," the conductor told me to get off, as the Château was on the opposite side, a little farther up the hill.

I went up the steps of the Château and banged on the great iron knocker. No one answered. So I pushed the huge heavy door open—it was not locked—and went in. The place seemed entirely deserted and empty, and so old and musty, even the stairs seeming crooked and shaky. I wandered about until finally I came to a door on the second floor, with a card nailed on it, bearing the name: "Count von Hatzfeldt."

I knocked, and the funniest little old man opened the door, and stood blinking at me.

"Count von Hatzfeldt?" I inquired.

Ceremoniously he bowed, and holding the door open, ushered me in. He had transformed that great room into a wonderful studio. It was at least five times the size of the average New York studio, considered extra large. From the beams in the ceiling hung a huge swing, and all about the walls and from the ceilings hung skins and things he had brought from Iceland, where he had lived for over six months with the Esquimaux, and he had ever so many paintings of the people.

I was intently interested and I wished my father could see the place. Count von Hatzfeldt showed me the work he was doing for the directors of the Château de Ramezay Society, who were intending to make a museum of the place. He was restoring the old portraits of the different Canadian governors and men of historical fame in Canada.

"I will want you to work on this Heraldry," he said, and indicated a long table scattered with water-color paper, water colors, and sketches of coats of arms. "I will sketch in the coat of arms, and you will do the painting, young lady. We use this gold and silver and bronze a great deal. This, I suppose, you know, is called 'painting *en gauche*.'"

I assured him I could do it. Papa had often painted in that medium, and had taught me. I told the Count that once a well-known artist of Boston called on papa to help him paint some fine lines on a big illustration. He said his eyes were bothering him, so he could not finish the work. It just happened that at that time papa's eyes were also troubling him, but as he did not want to lose the work, he had said:

"I'll send my little girl to you. She can do it better than I."

"And Count von Hatzfeldt," I said proudly, "I did do it, and the artist praised me when I finished the work, and he told papa he ought to send me to Boston to study at the art schools there."

At that time I was only thirteen. The Boston artist gave me ten dollars. I gave eight of it to mama. With the other two, I bought fifty cents' worth of candy, which I divided among all of us, mama included.

With the dollar-fifty left, I bought Ellen a birthday present of a brooch with a diamond as big as a pea in it that cost twenty-five cents. Then Ellen and I went to St. Helen's Island, and there we ate peanuts, drank spruce beer (a French-Canadian drink), had two swings and three merry-go-rounds, and what with the ten cents each for the ferry there was nothing left to pay our carfare home. So we walked, and mama was angry with us for being so late. She slapped Ellen for "talking back," and I always got mad if Ellen got hurt, so I "talked back" worse and then I got slapped, too, and we both had to go to bed without supper.

I didn't tell all this to the Count; only the first part about doing the work, etc. He said—he talked with a queer sort of accent, like a German, though I believe he was Scandinavian:

"Ya, ya! Vell, I will try you then. Come you to vork to-morrow and if you do vell, you shall have five dollar a veek. For that you vill vork on the coat of arms two hours a day, and if I find you can help me mit the portraits—it maybe you can lay in the bag-grounds, also the clothes—if so, I vill pay you some little more. Ya, ya!"

He rubbed his hands and smiled at me. He looked so much like a funny little hobgoblin that I felt like laughing at him, but there was also something very serious and almost angry in his expression.

"Now," said he, "the pusiness talk it is all done. Ya, ya!"

He said "Ya, ya!" constantly when he was thinking.

"I have met your good papa," he went on, "and I like him much. He is a man of great gift, but—"

He threw out his hands expressively.

"Poor papa," I thought. "I suppose he let the Count see how unbusiness-like and absent-minded he is."

After a moment the Count said:

"His—your papa's face—it is a typical northern one—such as we see plenty in Scandinavia—Ya, ya!"

"Papa is half-Irish and half-English," I explained.

He nodded.

"Ya, ya, it is so. Nevertheless his face is northern. It is typical, while you—" He regarded me smilingly. "Gott! You look like one little Indian girl that I meet when I live in the North. Her father, the people told me, was one big rich railway man of Canada, but he did not know that pretty little Indian girl, she was his daughter. Ya, ya!"

He rubbed his hands, and nodded his head musingly, as he studied me. Then:

"Come, I will show you the place here."

Pulling aside a curtain covering a large window (the Count shut out all the light except the north light), he showed me the great panorama of the city below us. We looked across the St. Lawrence River, and in the street directly below was the old Bonsecour market. I could see the carts of the "habitants" (farmers) loaded with vegetables, fruit and fresh maple syrup, some of it of the consistency of jelly. Never have I tasted such maple syrup since I left Canada. In the midst stood the old Bonsecour Church.

"Good people," it seemed to say, benevolently, "I am watching over you all!"

"It is," said the Count, "the most picturesque place in Montreal. Some day I will paint it, and then it shall be famous. Ya, ya! At present it is convenient to get the good things to eat. I take me five or ten cents in my hand, and those good habitants they give me so much food I cannot use it all. You vill take lunch with me, Ya, ya! and we will have the visitors here in the Château de Ramezal. Ya, ya!"

He had kept on tap two barrels of wine, which he bought from the Oke monks. He said they made a finer wine than any produced in this country or the United States. They made it from an old French recipe and sold it for a mere song. These monks, he told me, also made cheese and butter, and the cheese, he said, was better than the best imported. I used to see these monks on the street, and even in the coldest days in winter they wore only sandals on their feet, and their bare heads were shaved bald on top. They owned an island down the St. Lawrence, and depended on its products for their existence.

XIII

To my surprise, Reggie was not at all pleased when I told him of the work I had secured. I had been so delighted, and papa thought it an excellent thing for me. He said the Count was a genius and I would learn a great deal from him. Reggie, however, looked glum and sulky and said in his prim English way:

"You are engaged to be married to me, and I don't want my wife to be a working girl."

"But, Reggie," I exclaimed, "I have been working at home, doing all kinds of painting for different people and helping papa."

"That's different," he said sulkily. "A girl can work at home without losing her dignity, but when she goes out—well, she's just a working girl, that's all. Nice girls at home don't do it. My word! My people would take a fit if they thought I married a working girl. I've been trying to break it to them gradually about our engagement. I told them I knew very well a girl who was the granddaughter of Squire Ascough of Macclesfield, but I haven't had the nerve yet to tell them—to—er—"

I knew what he meant. He hadn't told them about us here, how poor we were, of our large family, and how we all had to work.

"I don't care a snap about your old people," I broke in heatedly, "and you don't have to marry me, Reggie Bertie. You can go back to England and marry the girl they want you to over there. (He had told me about her.) And, anyway, I'm sick and tired of your old English prejudices and notions, and you can go right now—the sooner the better. I hate you."

The words had rushed out of me headlong. I was furious at Reggie and his people. He was always talking about them, and I had been hurt and irritated by his failure to tell them about me. If he were ashamed of me and my people I wanted nothing to do with him, and now his objecting to my working made me indignant and angry.

Reggie, as I spoke, had turned deathly white. He got up as if to go, and slowly picked up his hat. I began to cry, and he stood there hesitating before me.

"Marion, do you mean that?" he asked huskily.

I said weakly:

"N-no, b-but I sha'n't give up the work. I gave up acting for you, but I won't my painting. I've *got* to work!"

Reggie drew me down to the sofa beside him.

"Now, old girl, listen to me. I'll not stop your working for this Count, but I want you to know that it's because I love you. I want my wife to be able to hold her head up with the best in the land, and none of our family—none of our women folk—have ever worked. As far as that goes, jolly few of the men have. I never heard of such a thing in our family."

"But there's no disgrace in working. Poor people have to do it," I protested. "Only snobs and fools are ashamed of it. Look at those Sinclair girls. They were all too proud to work, and their brother had to support them for years, and all the time he was in love with Ivy Lee and kept her waiting and waiting, and then she fell in love with that doctor and ran away and married him, and when Will Sinclair heard about it, he went into his room and shot himself dead. And it was all because of those big, strong, lazy sisters and vain, proud old mother, who were always talking about their noble family. All of us girls have got to work. Do you think we want poor old papa to kill himself working for us big, healthy young animals just because we happen to be girls instead of boys?"

Reggie said stubbornly:

"Nevertheless, it's not done by nice people, Marion. It's not proper, you know."

I pushed him away from me.

"Oh, you make me sick," I said.

"My brother-in-law, Wallace Burrows, would call that sort of talk rank snobbery. In the States women think nothing of working. They are proud to do it, women of the best families."

Reggie made a motion of complete distaste. The word "States" was always to Reggie like a red rag to a bull.

"My dear Marion, are you going to hold up the narsty Yankees as an example to me? My word, old girl! And as for that brother-in-law of yours, I say, he's hardly a gentleman, is he? Didn't you say the fellow was a—er—journalist or something like that?"

I jumped to my feet.

"He's a better kind of gentleman than you are!" I cried. "He's a genius, and—and—and—How dare you say anything about him! We all love him and are proud of him."

I felt my breath coming and going and my fist doubling up. I wanted to *pummel* Reggie just then.

"Come, come, old girl," he said. "Don't let's have a narsty scene. My word, I wouldn't quarrel with you for worlds. Now, look here, darling, you shall do as you like, and even if the governor cuts me off, I'll not give up my sweetheart."

He looked very sweet when he said that, and I melted in an instant. All of my bitterness and anger vanished. Reggie's promise to stand by me in spite of his people appealed to me as romantic and fine.

"Oh, Reggie, if they do cut you off, will you work for me with your hands?" I cried excitedly.

"My word, darling, how could I?" he exclaimed. "I'm blessed if I could earn a tuppence with them. Besides, I could hardly do work that was unbecoming a gentleman, now could I, darling?"

I sighed.

"I suppose not, Reggie, but do you know, I believe I'd love you lots more if you were a poor beggar. You're so much richer than I am now, and somehow—somehow—you seem sort of selfish, and as if you could never understand how things are with us. You seem—always—as if you were looking down on us. Ada says you think we aren't as good as you are."

"Oh, I say, Marion, that's not fair. I've always said your father was a gentleman. Come, come!" he added peevishly, "don't let's argue, there's a good girl. It's so jolly uncomfortable, and just think, I sharn't be with you much longer, now."

He was to sail for England the following week. I was wearing his ring, a lovely solitaire. In spite of all his prejudices and his selfishness, Reggie had lots of lovable traits, and he was so handsome. Then, too, he was really very much in love with me, and was unhappy about leaving me.

The day before he went, he took me in his arms and said, jealously:

"Marion, if you ever deceive me, I will kill you and myself, too. I know I ought to trust you, but you're so devilishly pretty, and I can't help being jealous of every one who looks at you. What's more, you aren't a bit like the girls at home. You say and do really shocking things, and sometimes, do you know, I'm really alarmed about you. I feel as if you might do something while I'm away that wouldn't be just right, you know."

I put my hand on my heart and solemnly I swore never, never to deceive Reggie, and to be utterly true and faithful to him forever. Somehow, as I spoke, I felt as if I were pacifying a spoiled child.

ONOTO WATANNA

XIV

All of that summer I worked for the old Count. Besides the Heraldry work, I assisted him with the restoration of the old oil portraits, some of which we had to copy completely. The Count had not much patience with the work the Society set him to do, and he let me do most of the copying, while he worked on other painting more congenial to him.

He was making a large painting of Andromeda, the figure of a nude woman tied to the rocks, and in the clouds was seen Perseus coming to deliver her. He had a very pretty girl named Lil Markey to pose for this.

My father was a landscape and marine painter, and never used models, and the first time I saw Lil I was repulsed and horrified. She came tripping into the studio without a stitch on her, and she even danced about and seemed to be amused by my shocked face. I inwardly despised her. Little did I dream that the time would come when I, too, would earn my living in that way.

I got much interested when I saw the Count painting from life. He tied Lil to an easel with soft rags, so as not to hurt her hands, and later he painted the rocks from a sketch, behind her, where the old easel was. While Lil rested, she would swing (still naked) in the big swing, and jump about and sing. In all my experiences later as an artist's model in America, I never saw a model who behaved as Lil did. The Count would give her cigarettes and she would tell stories that were not nice, and I had to pretend I didn't hear or couldn't understand them.

Lil was not exactly a bad girl, but sort of reckless and lacking entirely in modesty. She did have some decent homely traits, however. She would wrap a piece of drapery about her and say:

"You folks go on painting, and I'll be the cook."

Then she would disappear into the kitchen and come back presently with a delicious lunch which she had cooked all herself. I was afraid the Count was falling in love with her, for he used to look at her lovingly and sometimes he called her "Countess." Lil would make faces at him behind his back, and whisper to me: "Golly, he looks like a dying duck."

Twice a week, the Count had pupils, rich young women mostly, who learned to paint just as they did to play the piano and to dance. The Count would make fun of them to Lil and me. They would take a canvas and copy one of the Count's pictures, he doing most of the work. Then he would practically repaint it. The pupil, so the Count said, would then have it framed and when it was hung on the wall the proud parents would point to the work and admiring friends would say:

"What talent your daughter has!"

The Count, between chuckles and excited "Ya, ya's," would illustrate derisively the whole scene to Lil and me.

He tried to form a Bohemian club to meet at the studio in the Château, and we sent out many invitations for an opening party. When the evening came there was a large gathering of society folk, and we had the place full. Every one went looking at the Count's things and exclaiming about them, and they asked what he termed the "most foolish questions" about art.

Among them was a violinist, Karl Walter, whose exquisite music made me want to cry. He had a beautiful face, and I could not take my eyes from it all evening. When the party was over, he offered to see me home. The rest of the company were all departing in their carriages, and I thought rather drearily of that ride home on the horse-car. It seemed very short, however, with Mr. Walter. When we came to our door, he took my hand and said:

"Mademoiselle, I am going away for six months. When I return, I would like to know you better. Your sympathetic face was the only one I was playing to. The rest were all cattle."

He never came back to our Montreal, and I heard that he died soon after leaving us.

The morning after the party, the old Count was very irritable and cross, and when I asked him if he had enjoyed himself, he exclaimed disgustedly:

"Stupid! Stupid! Those Canadians, do not know the meaning of the word 'Bohemian.' It was a 'pink tea.' Ugh!"

I suggested that next time we should invite Patty Chase and Lu Fraser, and girls like that, but the Count shook his head with a hopeless gesture.

"That is the other extreme," he said. "No, no, you, my little friend, are the only one worthy to belong to such a club as I had hoped to start. It is impossible in this so stupid Canada."

XV

Rat-a-tat-tat, on the big iron knocker. I called:
"Come in," and Mrs. Wheatley, an English woman, accompanied by her daughter, Alice, a pretty girl of fifteen, entered. She came directly over to me, with her hand held out graciously.

"How do you do, Marion? I have been hearing about the Count, and I want you to introduce us."

I did so, of course, and she went on to tell the Count that she wanted her daughter's portrait painted.

"Just the head and shoulders, Count, and Miss Marion is here—her father and I are old friends—I shall not consider it necessary to come to the sittings. Marion will, I am sure, chaperon my little girl," and she smiled at me sweetly.

The Count was much pleased, and I could see his eyes sparkling as he looked at Alice. She was lovely, in coloring like a rose leaf, and her hair was a beautiful reddish gold. Her mother was a woman of about forty-five, rather plump, who affected babyish hats and fluffy dresses and tried to look younger than she was. After the Count had named a price she thought reasonable, she said Alice would come the next day. The Count was very gallant and polite to her and she seemed much impressed by his fine manners and I suppose, title.

"I have such a lovely old-gold frame, Count," she said, "and I thought Alice's hair would just match it and look lovely in it."

The Count threw up his hands and laughed when the door closed upon her, but he anticipated with pleasure painting the pretty Alice.

The following day Alice came alone, and soon we had her seated on the model's platform. She was a gentle, shy little thing, rather dull, yet so sweet and innocent that she made a most appealing picture. The Count soon discovered that her neck was as lovely as her face. In her innocence, Alice let him slip the drapery lower and lower until her girlish bosoms were partly revealed. The Count was charmed with her as a model. He made two pictures of her, one for himself, with her neck and breasts uncovered, and the other for her mother, muffled up with drapery to the neck.

A few weeks later, after the pictures were finished, I was crossing the street, when Mrs. Wheatley came rushing up to me excitedly:

"Miss Ascough! I am furious with you for allowing that wicked old Count to paint my Alice's portrait as I am told he did. Every one is talking about the picture in his studio. It is disgraceful! An outrage!"

"Oh, no, Mrs. Wheatley," I tried to reassure her, "it is not disgraceful, but beautiful, and the Count says that all beauty is good and pure and that is art, Mrs. Wheatley. Indeed, indeed, it is."

"Art! H'mph! The idea. Art! Do you think I want my Alice shown like those brazen hussies in the art galleries? I am surprised at you, Marion Ascough, and I advise you, for the sake of your family, to be more careful of your reputation. I am going right over to that studio now and I will put my parasol through that disgraceful canvas."

Fairly snorting with indignation and desire for vengeance, this British matron betook herself in the direction of the Château. Fortunately I was younger, and more fleet-footed than she, and I ran all of the way, and burst into the studio:

"Count Hatzfeldt! Count Hatzfeldt! Hurry up and hide Alice's picture. Mrs. Wheatley is coming to poke a hole in it."

Just as we were speaking, there came an impatient rap upon the door and the Count shoved his arms into the sleeves of his old velvet smoking-jacket, and himself flung the door open. Before Mrs. Wheatley, who was out of breath, could say a word, he exclaimed:

"How do you do it, madame? Heavens, it is vonderful, vonderful! How do you do it? Please have the goodness to tell me how you do it?"

"Do what?" she demanded, surprised and taken aback by the Count's evident admiration and cordiality.

"Why, madame, I thought you were your daughter. You look so young, so sweet, so fresh! Ah, madame, how I should love to paint you as the Spring! It is a treat for a poor artist to see so much freshness and peauty. Gott in Himmel! How do you do it?"

An astounding change had swept all over Mrs. Wheatley. She was simpering like a girl, and her eyes were flashing the most coquettish glances at the Count.

"Now, Count, you flatter me," she said, "but really I never do anything to make myself look younger. I simply take care of myself and lead a simple life. That is my only secret."

"Impossible," said the Count unbelievingly, and then his glance fell down to her feet and he exclaimed excitedly:

"What I have been looking for so many years! It is impossible to find a model with the perfect feets. Madame, you are vonderful!"

Her face was wreathed with smiles, and she stuck out her foot, the instep coyly arched, as she said:

"Yes, it's true my feet are shapely and small. I only take threes, though I could easily wear twos or twos and a half." Then with a very gracious bend of her head and a smile she added winningly: "I believe it might be perfectly proper to allow you to use my foot as a model, especially as Marion is here." She beamed on me sweetly.

I removed her shoe and stocking, and the Count carefully covered over a stool with a soft piece of velvet, upon which he set her precious foot. Enthusiastically he went to work drawing that foot. She playfully demanded that he must never tell anyone that her foot was the model for the sketch, though all the time I knew she wanted him to do just that.

When he was through and we had all loudly exclaimed over the beauty of the drawing, she said:

"And now, Count Hatzfeldt, may I see the copy of my daughter's picture?"

The Count had covered it over before opening the door.

"Certainly, madame."

He drew the cover from the painting.

"Here it is. Miss Alice did sit for the face. The lower part—it was posed by a professional model. It is the custom, madame."

"As I see," said Mrs. Wheatley, examining the picture through her lorgnon. "Those professional models have no shame, have they, Count?"

"None, none whatever, madame," sighed the Count, shaking his head expressively.

XVI

I had received, of course, a great many letters from Reggie, and I wrote to him every day. He expected to return in the fall, and he wrote that he was counting the days. He said very little in his letters about his people, though he must have known I was anxiously awaiting word as to how they had taken the news of our engagement.

Toward the end of summer, his letters came less frequently, and, to my great misery, two weeks passed away when I had not word from him at all. I was feeling blue and heartsick and, but for my work at the Château, I think I would have done something desperate. I was really tremendously in love with Reggie and I worried and fretted over his long absence and silence.

Then one day, in late September, a messenger boy came with a letter for me. It was from Reggie. He had returned from his trip, and was back in Montreal. Instead of being happy to receive his letter, I was filled with resentment and indignation. He should have come himself and, in spite of what he wrote, I felt I could not excuse him. This was his letter:

DARLING GIRLIE

I am counting the hours when I will be with you. I tried to get up to see you last night, but it was impossible. Lord Eaton's son, young Albert, was on the steamer coming over, and they are friends of the governor's and I simply had to be with them. You see, darling, it means a good deal to me in the future, to be in touch with these people. His brother-in-law, whom I met last night, is head cockalorum in the House of Parliament, and as I have often told you, my ambition is to get into politics. It's the surest road to fame for a Barrister.

Now I hope my foolish little girl will understand and believe me when I say that I am thinking for you as much as for myself.

I am hungry for a kiss, and I feel I cannot wait till tonight.

Your own,
REGGIE

ONOTO WATANNA

For the first time in my life I experienced the pangs of jealousy and yet I was jealous of something tangible. It was lurking in my thought, and all sorts of suspicions and fears came into my hot head.

When Reggie came that evening I did not open the door as usual. I heard him say eagerly, when the children let him in:

"Where's Marion?"

I was peeping over the banister, and I deliberately went back into the bedroom and counted five hundred before I went down to see him.

He was walking excitedly up and down and as I came in he sprang to meet me, his arms outstretched; but I drew back coldly. Oh, how bitter I felt, and vindictive, too!

"How do you do, Mr. Bertie," I said.

"Mr. Bertie! Marion, what does this mean?"

He stared at me incredulously, and then I saw a look of amazement and suspicion come into his face, which had grown suddenly red as with rage.

"Good God!" he cried. "Do you mean you don't care for me any more? Then you must be in love with someone else."

"Reggie," I sneered, "don't try to cover up your own falseness by accusing me. You pretend to love me, and yet after all these months when you get back, you do not come to *me*, but go to see other women (I was guessing) and men."

I ended with a sob of rage, for I could see in Reggie's face that my surmises were correct. He, however, exclaimed:

"Oh, that's it, is it?" And before I could move, he had seized me impulsively in his arms and was kissing me again and again. I never *could* resist Reggie once he got his arms about me. I always became just as weak as a kitten and I think I would have believed anything he told me then. I just melted to him, as it were. He knew it well, the power of his strong arms about me, and whenever he wanted his way about anything with me he would pick me right up and hold me till I gave in. After a moment, with me still in his arms, he said:

"It's true I was with men and women, but that was not my fault. There's such a thing as duty. I had no pleasure in their society. I was longing for you all the time, but I had to stay with them because they are influential people, and I want to use them to help me—us, Marion."

"Who were those women?" I demanded.

"Only some friends of my family's. They had a box at the theatre, and there was young Eaton, of course, and his sister and a cousin. They bored me to death, give you my word they did, darling. Come, come now, be good to your tired old Reggie."

I was glad to make up with him and, oh! infinitely happy to have him back. The great oceans of water that had been between us seemed to have melted away. Nevertheless, he had planted a feeling in me that I could not entirely rid myself of, a feeling of distrust. Like a weed, it was to grow in my heart to terrible proportions.

XVII

The days that followed were happy ones for me. Reggie was with me constantly, and I even got off several afternoons from the studio and spent the time with him.

One day we made a little trip up the St. Lawrence, Reggie rowing all the way from the wharf at Montreal to Boucherville. We started at noon and arrived at six. There we tied up our boat and went to look for a place for dinner. We found a little French hotel and Reggie said to the proprietor:

"We want as good a dinner as you can give us. We've rowed all the way from Montreal and are famished."

"Bien! You sall have ze turkey which is nearly cook," said the hotel keeper. "M'sieu he row so far. It is too much. Only Beeg John, ze Indian, row so far. He go anny deestance. Also he go in his canoe down those Rapids of Lachine. Vous connais dat man—Beeg John?"

Yes, we knew about him. Every one in Montreal did.

We waited on the porch while he prepared our dinner. The last rays of the setting sun were dropping down in the wood, and away in the distance the reflections upon the St. Lawrence were turning into dim purple the brilliant orange of a little while ago. Never have I seen a more beautiful sunset than that over our own St. Lawrence. I said wistfully:

"Reggie, the sunset makes me think of this poem:

> *"The sunset gates were opened wide,*
> *Far off in the crimson west,*
> *As through them passed the weary day*
> *In rugged clouds to rest."*

Before I could finish the last line, Reggie bent over and kissed me right on the mouth.

"Funny little girl," he said. "Suppose instead of quoting poetry you speak to me, and instead of looking at sunsets, you look at me."

"Reggie, don't you like poetry then?"

"It's all right enough, I suppose, but I'd rather have straight English words. What's the sense of muddling one's language? Silly, I call it," he said.

I felt disappointed. Our family had always loved poetry. Mama used to read Tennyson's "Idyls of the King," and we knew all of the characters, and even played them as children. Moreover, papa and Ada and Charles and even Nora could all write poetry. Ada made up poems about every little incident in our lives. When papa went to England, mama would make us little children all kneel down in a row and repeat a prayer to God that she had made up to send him back soon. Ada wrote a lovely poem about God hearing us. She also wrote a poem about our Panama hen who died. She said the wicked cock hen, a hen we had that could crow like a cock, had killed her. How we laughed over that poem. I was sorry Reggie thought it was nonsense, and I wished he would not laugh or sneer at all the things we did and liked.

"Dinner is ready pour m'sieu et madame!"

Gracious! That man thought I was Reggie's wife. I colored to my ears, and I was glad Reggie did not understand French.

He had set the table for two and there was a big sixteen pound turkey on it, smelling so good and looking brown and delicious. I am sure our Canadian turkeys are better than any I have ever tasted anywhere else. They certainly are not "cold-storage birds."

They charged Reggie for that whole sixteen-pound turkey. He thought it a great joke, but I wanted to take the rest home. The tide being against us, we left the rowboat at the hotel with instructions to return it, and we took the train back to Montreal.

Coming home on the train, the conductor proved to be a young man who had gone to school with me and he came up with his hand held out:

"Hallo, Marion!"

"Hallo, Jacques."

I turned to Reggie to introduce him, but Reggie was staring out of the window and his chin stuck out as if it were in a bad temper. When Jacques had passed along, I said crossly to Reggie:

"You needn't be so rude to my friends, Reggie Bertie."

"Friends!" he sneered. "My word, Marion, you seem to have a passion for low company."

I said:

"Jacques is a nice, honest fellow."

"No doubt," said Reggie loftily. "I'll give him a tip next time he passes."

"Oh, how *can* you be so despicably mean?" I cried.

He turned around in his seat abruptly:

"What in the world has come over you, Marion! You have changed since I came back."

I felt the injustice of this and shut my lips tight. I did not want to quarrel with Reggie, but I was burning with indignation and I was hurt through and through by his attitude.

In silence we left the train and in silence went to my home. At the door Reggie said:

"We had a pleasant day. Why do you always spoil things so? Good-night."

I could not speak. I had done nothing and he made me feel as if I had committed a crime. The tears ran down my face and I tried to open the door. Reggie's arms came around me from behind, and, tilting back my face, he kissed me.

"There, there, old girl," he said, "I'll forgive you this time, but don't let it happen again."

XVIII

I had finished the work for the Château de Ramezay, but the Count said I could stay on there, and that he would try to help me get outside work. He did get me quite a few orders for work of a kind he himself would not do.

One woman gave me an order to paint pink roses on a green plush piano cover. She said her room was all in green and pink. When I had finished the cover, she ordered a picture "of the same colors." She wished me to copy a scene of meadows and sheep. So I painted the sunset pink, the meadows green and the sheep pink. She was delighted and said it was a perfect match to her carpets.

The Count nearly exploded with delight about it. My orders seemed to give him exquisite joy and he sometimes said, to see me at work compensated for much and made life worth while. He used to hover about me, rubbing his hands and chuckling to himself and muttering: "Ya, ya!"

I did a lot of decorating of boxes for a manufacturer and painted dozens of sofa pillows. Also I put "real hand-painted" roses on a woman's ball dress, and she told me it was the envy of every one at the big dance at which she wore it.

I did not love these orders, but I made a bit of money, and I needed clothes badly. It was impossible to go around with Reggie in my thin and shabby things. Moreover, an especially cold winter had set in and I did want a new overcoat badly. I hated to have to wear my old blanket overcoat. It looked so dreadfully Canadian, and many a time I have seen Reggie look at it askance, though, to do him justice, he never made any comment about my clothes. In a poor, large family like ours, there was little enough left for clothes.

About the middle of winter, the Count began to have bad spells of melancholia. He would frighten me by saying:

"Some day ven you come in the morning, you vill find me dead. I am so plue, I vish I vas dead."

I tried to laugh at him and cheer him up, but every morning as I came through those ghostly old halls, I would think of the Count's words and I would be afraid to open the door.

One day, about five in the afternoon, when I was getting ready to go, the Count who was sitting near the fire all hunched up, said:

"Please stay mit me a little longer. Come sit by me a little vile. Your radiant youth vill varm me up."

I had an engagement with Reggie and was in a hurry to get away. So I said:

"I can't, Count. I've got to run along."

He stood up suddenly and clicked his heels together.

"Miss Ascough," he said, "I think after this, you better vork some other place. You have smiles for all the stupid Canadian poys, but you vould not give to me the leastest."

"Why, Count," I said, astonished, "don't be foolish. I'm in a hurry to-night, that's all. I've an engagement."

"Very vell, Miss Ascough? Hurry you out. It is pest you come not pack again."

"Oh, very well!" I said. "Good-bye." I ran down the stairs, feeling much provoked with the foolish old fellow.

Poor old Count! How I wish I had been kinder and more grateful to him; but in my egotistical youth I was incapable of hearing or understanding his pathetic call for sympathy and companionship. I was flying along through life, as we do in youth. I was, indeed, as I had said, "in a hurry."

He died a few years later in our Montreal, a stranger among strangers, who saw only in the really beauty-loving soul of the artist the grotesque and queer. I wished then that I could have been with him in the end, but I myself was in a strange land, and I was experiencing some of the same appalling loneliness that had so oppressed and crushed my old friend.

XIX

When I told Reggie I was not going to the Château any more, he was very thoughtful for some time. Then he said:

"Why don't you take a studio up town? You can't do anything in this God-forsaken Hochelaga."

"Why, Reggie," I said, "you talk as if a studio were to be had for nothing. Where can I find the money to pay the rent?"

"Look here," said he, "I'm sure to pass my finals this spring, and I'm awfully busy. It takes a deuce of a time to get down here. Now if you had a studio of your own it would be perfectly proper for me to see you there, and then, besides, don't you see, darling, I would have you all to myself? Here we are never alone hardly, unless I take you out."

"I couldn't afford to pay for such a place," I said, sighing, for I would have loved to have a studio of my own.

"Tell you what you do," said Reggie. "You let me pay for the room. You needn't get an expensive place, you know—just a little studio. Then you tell your governor that you get the room free for teaching or painting for the landlady, or something like that. What do you say, darling?"

"I thought you said you despised a lie?" was my answer. "You said you would never forgive me if I deceived you or told you a lie."

"But that was to me, darling. That's different. It's not lying exactly—just using a bit of diplomacy, don't you see?"

"I'm afraid I can't do it, Reggie. I ought to stay at home. They really need my help, now Ellen and Charles are both married, and Nellie engaged and may marry any time."

Nellie was the girl next to me. She was engaged to a Frenchman who was urging her to marry right away.

"You see," I went on, "there's only Ada helping. The other girls are too young to work yet, though Nora is leaving home next week."

"Nora! That kid! What on earth is she going to do?"

"Oh, Nora's not so young. She's nearly seventeen. You forget we've been engaged some time now, and all the children are growing up."

I said this sulkily. Secretly I resented Reggie's constantly putting off our marriage day.

"But what is *she* going to do?"

"Oh, she's going out to the West Indies. She's got a position on some paper out there."

"Whee!" Reggie drew a long whistle. "West Indies! I'll be jiggered if your parents aren't the easiest ever. Your mother is the last woman in the world to bring up a family of daughters, and I'm blessed if I ever came across any father like yours. Why, do you know when I asked him for his consent to our engagement, he never asked me a single question about myself, but began to talk about his school days in France, and how he walked when he was a boy from Boulogne to Calais. When I pushed him for an answer, he said absently, 'Yes, yes, I suppose it's all right, if she wants you,' and the next moment asked me if I had read Darwin."

Reggie laughed heartily at the memory, and then he said:

"Yet I'm fond of your governor, Marion. He is a gentleman."

"Dear papa," I said, "wouldn't hurt a fly, but anybody could cheat him, and that is why I hate to deceive him."

"Well, don't lie to him then if you feel that way. Just say you are going to take a studio up town and I bet you anything he'll never bother his head where you go or how you pay the rent. As for your mother, if you told her the studio was free, she would think that just the usual thing and that you were doing the landlord an honor in using it."

Again Reggie burst out laughing, but I would not laugh with him, so he stopped and said:

"Your mother's awfully proud of you, darling, and I don't blame her. She told me one day that you were the most beautiful baby in England, where she said you were born. She said she used to take you out to show you off, as were her show child. Your mother is a joke, there's no mistake about that. And to think you are afraid to leave them to go up town! Come, come darling, don't be a little goose. Think how cozy it will be for us both!"

It would be "cozy." I realized that, and then the thought of having a studio all to myself appealed to me. Reggie and I were engaged, and why should I not let him do a little thing like that to help me. Reggie had never been a very generous lover. The presents he made me were few and far between, and often I had secretly compared his affluent appearance with my own shabby self. After all, I could get a room for a fairly nominal price, and perhaps if I got plenty of work, I would soon be able to pay for it myself. So I agreed to look for a place, much to Reggie's delight.

As Reggie had predicted, papa and mama were not particularly interested when I told them I was going to open a studio up town, and even when I added that I might not be able to come home every night, but would sleep sometimes on a lounge in the studio mama merely said:

"Well, you must be sure to be home for Sunday dinners anyway."

Ada, however, looked up sharply and said:

"How much will it cost you?"

I stammered and said I did not know, but that I would get a cheap place. Ada then said:

"Well, you ought to try and sell papa's paintings there, too. Nobody wants to come to Hochelaga to look at them."

I replied eagerly that I would show papa's work, and I added that I was going to try and start a class in painting, too.

"If you make any money," said Ada, "you ought to help the family, as I have been doing for some time now, and you are much stronger than I am, and almost as old."

Ada had been delicate from a child, and already I was taller and larger than she. She made up in spirit what she lacked in stature. She was almost fanatically loyal to mama and the family. She devoted herself to them and tried to imbue in all of us the same spirit of pride.

XX

L u Frazer went with me to look for a room. Lu was an Irish-Canadian girl with whom I had gone to school. She worked as a stenographer for an insurance firm, and was very popular with all the girls. There was something about her that made nearly all the girls go to her and consult her about this or that, and tell her all about their love affairs.

I think the attraction lay in Lu's absolute interest in others. She never talked about her own feelings or affairs, but was always willing to listen to the outpourings of others. When you told her anything she was full of sympathetic murmurs, or screams of joy, or expressions of indignation if the story you told her called for that.

I had formed the habit of going to Lu about all my worries and anxieties over Reggie, and I always found a willing listener and staunch champion. The girls called her the Irish Jew, as she kept a bank account and whenever the girls were short of money they would borrow from Lu, who would charge them interest. Reggie heartily disliked her without any just reason. He said:

"She belongs to a class that should by right be scrubbing floors; only she got some schooling, so she is ticking the typewriter instead."

Nevertheless, I liked Lu, and in spite of Reggie kept her as my friend, though she knew that he hated her. When I told her about Reggie's offer to pay for the studio, she said:

"Um! Then take as fine a one as you can get, Marion. Soak him good and hard. I hear he pays a great big price for his own rooms at the Windsor."

I explained to her that I only wanted as cheap a place as I could get, and that as soon as I made enough money, I intended to pay for it myself.

We looked through the advertisements in the papers, made a list and then went forth to look for that "studio."

On Victoria Street, we found a nice big front parlor which seemed to be just what I wanted. The landlady offered it to me for ten dollars a month, and when I said that that would do nicely she asked if I were alone, and when I said I was, she said:

"I hope you work out all day."

I told her I worked in my room, and that I would make a studio out of it. Whereupon she said:

"I prefer ladies who go out to work. I had one lady here before, and I had to put her out. She stayed in bed till eleven and I found cigarette ashes in her room. Then she had some gentlemen callers, and they actually shut the door. As this is a respectable house, I went into the back parlor and watched her through a crack in the folding doors. Then I goes back and raps on the door, and I says: 'Young person'—I wouldn't call the likes of her a lady—I says: 'Young person, I want my room. I'm a lone widow woman and I have to consider my reputation, and the carryings on in that room is what I won't have in my house.' So out she goes. I am a lady, even if I do keep a rooming-house."

I looked at Lu, and Lu said:

"We'll call again."

"Oh," said the woman, "if you decide to take this room I'll make a reduction, and I don't mind gentlemen callers if you leave the door open."

I felt a sort of disgust come over me and, telling her I did not want the room, I made for the door, hurrying Lu along.

"Oh, I see," she shouted after us, "you want to *shut* the door!"

After looking about, we found a back parlor in a French-Canadian house on University Street. The landlady was very polite, and I paid her eight dollars in advance.

The following day I moved all my things into the "studio," as it now, in fact, began to look like, what with all my paintings about and some of papa's, an easel, palette and painting materials. I covered up the ugly couch with some draperies the Count sent over for me. Poor old fellow, he had sent word to me the very next day to come back, saying he missed his little pupil very much, but at Reggie's advice I wrote him that I had taken a studio of my own. He then sent me a lot of draperies and other things, and wrote that he would come to see me very soon.

I had a sign painted on black japanned tin, with the following inscription:

Miss Marion Ascough
Artist
Orders taken for all kinds of work.

I got the landlady to put it in the front window.

There were a lot of crayon family portraits on my walls, and they looked very bad. I covered them over with draperies, and when Madame Lavalle, my landlady, came in she exclaimed:

"Why you dat? Am I and my family so hugly then?"

I assured her that I covered them to protect them from the turpentine that I used in my oil paints. She came to me later and said:

"Mamselle, I am tell my husband you say the turpentine it may be will spoil the portraits of my familee. He's telling me dat will not spoil it. But if mamselle will not be offend, I the pictures will put in my own parlor, and if some time mamselle she have company, and wish her room to look more elegant, I will give ze permission to hang them on her walls again."

The studio was all settled, and I stood to survey my work, a delightful feeling of proprietorship coming over me. I breathed a sigh of blessed relief to think I was now free of all home influence, and had a real place all of my own.

"Here is some gentlemens to see mamselle," called Madame Lavalle, and there standing in the doorway, smiling at me with a merry twinkle in his eye, was Colonel Stevens. I had not seen him since that night, nearly four years ago, when Ellen and I went to ride with him in Mr. Mercier's carriage. With him now was a tall man with a very red face and nose. He wore a monocle in his eye, and he was staring at me through it.

I was very untidy as I had been busy settling up, and my hair was all mussed up and my hands dirty. I had on my painting apron, and that was smudged over, too. I felt ashamed of my appearance, but Colonel Stevens said:

"Isn't she cute?"

Then he introduced us. His friend's name was Davidson.

"We were on our way to the Club," said the Colonel, "and as we passed your place I saw your sign, and 'By Gad,' I said, 'I believe that is my little friend, Marion.' Now Mr. Davidson is very much interested in art." He gave a little wink at Mr. Davidson, and then went on, "and I think he wants to buy some of your paintings."

"Oh, sit down," I urged. Customers at once! I was excited and happy. I pushed out a big armchair near the fire and Colonel Stevens sat down, and seemed very much at home. Mr. Davidson followed me to where I had a number of little paintings on a shelf. I began to show them to him, pointing out the places, but he scarcely looked at them. Stretching out his hand, he picked up two and said:

"I'll take these. How much am I to give you?"

"Oh, five—" I began.

"Charge him the full price, Marion," put in the Colonel. "He's a rich dog."

"I get five dollars for two of that size," I said.

"Well, we'll turn it to ten for each," smiled Mr. Davidson.

"Oh, that's too much!" I exclaimed.

"Tut, tut!" said Colonel Stevens, laughing. "They are worth more. She really is a very clever little girl, eh, Davidson?"

I felt uncomfortable and to cover my confusion I started to wrap the paintings.

"No, no, don't bother," said Mr. Davidson, "leave them here for the present. I'll call another time for them. We have to go now."

When Mr. Davidson shook hands with me he pressed my hand so that I could hardly pull it away, and just as they were passing out, who should come up the stairs but Reggie! When he saw Colonel Stevens and Mr. Davidson, his face turned perfectly livid, and he glared at them. The minute the door had closed upon them, he turned on me:

"What were those men doing here?" he demanded harshly.

My face got hot, and I felt guilty, though of what, I did not know.

"Well? Why don't you answer me? What was that notorious libertine, Stevens, and that beast, Davidson, doing here?" he shouted, and then as still I did not answer him, he yelled: "Why don't you answer me instead of standing there and staring at me, looking your guilt? God in heaven! have I been a fool about you? Have you been false to me then?"

"No, Reggie, indeed, I haven't," I said. "I didn't tell you about Ellen and I going out with him because—because—"

I thought he must have heard of that ride!

"Going out with him! When? Where?"

Suddenly he saw the money in my hand, and the sight of it seemed to drive him wild.

"What are you doing with that money? Where did you get it from?"

I was holding the two ten-dollar bills all the time in my hand.

"Are you crazy, Reggie?" I cried. "How can you be so silly? This is the money Mr. Davidson paid me for these paintings."

"Well, then, what are you doing here if he bought them?" demanded Reggie.

"He left them here. He said he'd call some other time for them."

"Marion, are you a fool, or just a deceitful actress? Can't you see he does not want your paintings? He gave you that money for expected favors and, damn it! I believe you know it too."

I went over to Reggie, and somehow felt older than he. A great pity for him filled my heart. I put my arms around his neck, and although he tried to push me from him, I stuck to him and then suddenly, to my surprise, Reggie began to cry. He had worked himself up to such a state of excitement that he was almost hysterical. I gathered his head to my breast, and cried with him.

In a little while, we were sitting in the big armchair and I told Reggie all about the visit, and also about that ride of long ago—before I had even met him—that Ellen and I had taken with Colonel Stevens and Mr. Mercier. I think he was ashamed of himself, but was too stubborn to admit it. Before he left, he made a parcel of those two paintings, and sent them over, with a bill receipted by me, to the St. James Club.

XXI

It was snowing hard. The snow was coming down in great big flakes. I had built a big fire in my grate and had turned off all the gas lights. The flames from the grate threw their glare upon the walls. I was waiting for Reggie, and I was wondering where I was going to get some money to pay for clothes I badly needed now, but out of the little I had been earning I had been obliged to send most of it home. It seemed to me as if every time Ada came to see me, it was as a sort of collector. Help was needed at home, and Ada was going to see that we all did our share.

I had had my studio now some time and I had made very little money. Reggie had paid the rent each month, but I had never taken any other help from Reggie. He seemed to have so much money to spend, and yet he was always saying he was too poor to marry though he had passed his examinations and was a full partner in the big law firm. He said he wanted to build up a good practice before we married.

I heard his footsteps in the hall and the door opened.

"Hallo, hallo! Sitting all alone in the dark, darling?"

Reggie came happily into the studio. He was in evening dress with his rich fur-lined coat thrown open. He sat down on the arm of my chair.

"I'm awfully disappointed, darling," he said. "I had been looking forward to spending the evening here by the fire with you, but I'm obliged to go with my partners and a party of friends to a dinner they are giving, and I expect to meet that member of Parliament I told you about. If I can break away early, I'll come back here and say good-night to the sweetest girl in the world. So don't go home to-night, as we can have a few moments together anyway."

I was left once more alone. I sat there staring into the fire. Why did Reggie never take me to these dinners? There were always women there. Why was I not introduced to his friends? Why did he leave me more and more alone like this? He was jealous of every man who spoke to me, and yet he left me alone and went to dinners and parties where he did not think I was good enough to go.

Some one was rapping on the door, and I called:

"Come!"

It was Lu Frazer.

"Why, Marion Ascough, what are you sitting alone in the dark for? Where is the fair one of the golden locks?"

Lu was shaking the snow from her clothes, but she stopped suddenly when she saw my face.

"What are you crying about?"

"I'm not crying. I'm just yawning."

Lu put her hands on my shoulders.

"What's his nibs been saying to you now?" she asked.

I shook my head. Somehow I didn't feel like confiding even in Lu this night.

"Look here, Marion," she said, "I met an old admirer of yours as I came here to-night, and he asked me to try and get you to go with him and a friend to a little supper. He said you knew his friend—that he'd bought some pictures from you. His name's Davidson. Folks do say that his father was the Prince of Wales and that he got fresh with one of the Davidson girls that time when he was in Canada and their father entertained him, and they pass this Davidson off as a younger son of the family. I told Colonel Stevens I'd do what I could. Now, I saw that Bertie getting into a sleigh all rigged up in evening clothes and with that Mrs. Marbridge and her sister. Folks are saying he's paying attention to the latter lady. I said to myself, when I saw him: 'What's sass for the goose is sass for the gander.' Marion, you're a fool to sit moping here, while he is enjoying himself with other women."

I jumped to my feet.

"I'll go with you, Lu—anywhere. I'm crazy to go with you. Let's hurry up."

"All right, get dressed while I 'phone the Colonel. He said he'd be waiting at the St. James Club for an answer for the next half-hour."

I HAVE A VERY DIM remembrance of that evening. We were in some restaurant, and the drink was cold and yet it burned my throat like fire. I had never tasted any liquor before, except the light wine that the Count sometimes sparingly gave me. I heard some one saying—I think it was Mr. Davidson:

"She's a hell of a girl to take out for a good time."

I said I felt ill, and Lu took me out to get the air. She said she would be back soon. But once out there, I conceived a passionate desire to return to my room and I ran away in the street from Lu.

As I opened my door a feeling of calamity seemed to come over me. It must have been nearly twelve o'clock, and I had never been out so late before, not even with Reggie.

As I came in, Reggie, who had been sitting by the table, stood up. He stared at me for a long time without saying a word. Then:

"You've been out with men!" he said.

"Yes," I returned defiantly, "I have."

"And you've been drinking!"

"Yes," I said. "So have you."

He flung me from him, and then all of a sudden he threw himself down in the chair by the table and, putting his head upon his arms, he shook with sobs. All of my anger melted away and I knelt down beside him and entreated him to forgive me. I told him just where I had been and with whom, and I said that it was all because I was tired, tired of waiting so long for him. I said:

"Reggie, no man has a right to bind a girl to a long engagement like this. Either marry me, or set me free. I am wasting my life for you."

He said if we were to be married now, his whole future would be ruined; that he expected to be nominated to a high political position, and to marry at this stage of his career would be sheer madness.

I promised to wait for Reggie one more year; but I was very unhappy, and all the rest of that winter I could not refrain from constantly referring to our expected marriage, though I knew it irritated him for me to refer to it.

XXII

My younger sister, Nellie, had married her Frenchman. The family began to look upon me as they did on Ada, as an old maid! And I was only twenty-one.

Reggie had been much wrapped up in certain elections and I had seen him only for a few minutes each day, when one night he came over to the studio. He looked very handsome and reckless. I think he had been drinking, for there was a strange look about his eyes, and when he took me in his arms I thought he was never going to let me go. Whenever Reggie was especially kind to me, I always thought it a good time to broach the subject of our marriage. So now I said:

"Reggie, don't you think it would be lovely if we could arrange to be married in June? I hate to think of another summer alone."

It was a clear, sweet night in April, and my windows were all open. There was the fragrance of growing green in the air, and it seemed as warm as an early summer day. I felt happy, and oh, so drawn to my handsome Reggie as he held me close in his arms. He put his warm face right down on mine, and he said:

"Darling girl, if we were to marry, you cannot imagine the mess it would make of my career. My father would never forgive me. Don't you see my whole future might be ruined? Be my wife in every way but the silly ceremony. If you loved me, you would make this sacrifice for me."

Something snapped in my head! I pushed him from me with my hands doubled into fists. For the first time I saw Reginald Bertie clearly! My sister was right. He was a monument of selfishness and egotism. He was worse. He was a beast who had taken from me all my best years, and now—*now* he made a proposition to me that was vile!—me, the girl he had asked to be his wife! What had I done, then, that he should have changed like this to me? I was guilty of no fault, save that of poverty. I knew that had I been possessed of those things that Reggie prized so much, never would he have insulted me like this.

I felt him approaching me with his arms held out, but I backed away from him and suddenly I found myself hysterically speaking those lines from Camille. I was pointing to the door:

"That's your way!" I screamed at him. "Go!"

"Marion—darling—forgive me—I didn't mean that."

But I wouldn't listen to him, and when at last he was out of my room, I locked and bolted the door upon him.

XXIII

I did not sleep all of that night, and when the morning dawned I had made up my mind what to do.

I packed up all my things and then I went out to see Lu Frazer. I told her I was going to leave Montreal—that I wanted to go to the States—to Boston, where that artist had told papa I ought to study. I felt sure I would get work there, and could study besides. I borrowed twenty-five dollars from Lu, and promised to pay her back thirty-five within three months.

When I got back to my studio I found this letter from Reggie:

DARLING

I know you will forgive your heartbroken Reggie, who was not himself last night. All shall be as it was between us, and I swear to you that never again will I say anything to my little girl that will hurt her feelings.

Your repentant,
REGGIE

I crushed his letter up in my hand. I felt that my love for him was dead. I never wanted to see him again. He had sacrificed me for the sake of his selfish ambitions.

My train was to leave at eight, and Lu was going to be there to see me off. I sat down and wrote the following letter to Reggie before leaving the house:

DEAR REGGIE:

I am leaving for Boston tonight. I have loved you very dearly, and I feel bad at leaving you without saying good-bye, but I will not live any longer in that studio that you pay for, and I could not stand home any more.

I can earn my living better in Boston, and when you are ready I will come back to you, but I cannot trust myself to say good-bye.

Your loving,
MARION

Then I went down to Hochelaga and said good-bye to them all at home. Papa hunted up the address of Mr. Sands, that artist for whom I had done that work when a little girl of thirteen. Papa felt sure he would help me get something. Mama and papa seemed to have a vague idea that I had some definite place I could go to, and they did not ask any questions. We girls often felt older than our parents. Anyway, more worldly, and they had the greatest trust in our ability to take care of ourselves.

Ada thought it a good thing for me to go. She said I would get better pay for my work in Boston, and that I must be sure to send something home each week, just as Nora was doing.

I felt a lump in my throat when I left the old house. There was still a bit of snow in the garden, though it was April, where I had played as a child. I put my head out of the cab window to take a last look at the familiar places, which I told myself, with a sob, I might never see again.

Lu was at the station. She had my ticket, and the balance of the twenty-five dollars in an envelope which she slipped into my hand. The train was nearly due to go. My foot was on the step when I heard Reggie's voice calling my name. He came running down the platform:

"Marion! You shall not go. You're carrying this too far, darling."

"Yes, yes, I'm going," I said to Reggie. "You're not going to stop me any longer."

"But, Marion, I didn't mean what I said."

I stared up at him directly.

"Reggie, if I stay, will we be married—right away?"

"Why—Marion, look here, old girl, you can wait a little longer, can't you?"

I laughed up at him harshly.

"No!" I cried harshly, "I can't. And I hope God will never let me see your face again."

I ran up the steps of the train and started inside. I did not look out.

XXIV

Never shall I forget that journey in the train, I had not thought to get a sleeper, so I sat up all night long. I had the whole seat to myself. The conductor turned the next seat over toward me, and by putting up my feet, I was fairly comfortable.

I shut my eyes and tried to go to sleep, but the thoughts that came thronging through my head were too many. I wept for my lost sweetheart, and yet I vowed never to go back to him. His future should not be spoiled by me.

Oh, as I thought of how many times Reggie had said that, a feeling of helpless rage against him took possession of me. I saw him in all his ambitious, selfish, narrow snobbery and pride. Even his love for me was a part of his peculiar fastidiousness. He wanted me for himself because I was prettier than most girls, just as he wanted all luxurious things, but he never stopped to think of my comfort or happiness.

Somehow, as the train slipped farther and farther away from Montreal, Reggie's influence over me seemed to be vanishing, and presently, as I gazed out into the night, he passed away from my mind altogether.

We were passing through dark meadows, and they looked gloomy and mysterious under that starlit sky. I thought of how papa had taught us all so much about the stars, and how he said one of our ancestors had been a great astronomer. Ada knew all of the planets and suns by name and could pick them out, but to me they were always little points of mystery. I remembered as a little girl I used to look up at them and say to one particular star:

> *"Star bright, star light*
> *First star I see to-night,*
> *Wish I may—wish I might*
> *Get the wish I wish to-night."*

Then I would say quickly:

"Give me a doll's carriage."

Ada had told me if I did that for seven nights, the fairies would give me whatever I asked for, and each night I asked for that doll's carriage. I watched to see it come and I would say to Ada:

"What's the matter with that old fairy? I thought you said she'd give me my wish?"

Ada would answer:

"Oh, fairies are invisible, and no doubt the carriage is right near by, but you can't see it."

"But what's the use," I would say, "of a carriage I can't see?"

"Try it again," would say Ada. "Perhaps they'll relent. You probably offended them, or didn't do it just right."

For seven nights more, I would faithfully repeat the formula. Then at Ada's suggestion I would hunt in the tall grass at the end of the garden.

"Perhaps," Ada would say, "there is a fairy sitting on the edge of a blade of grass and she has the carriage."

Then I would lie in the grass and wait for the carriage to become visible. I never got that doll's carriage. The fairies never relented.

I dozed for a little while and was awakened by the faint crowing of cocks, and I thought sleepily of a little pet chicken I used to dress in baby's clothes, and I dreamed of a lovely wax doll that Mrs. McAlpin had given me.

It was queer how, as I lay there, all these little details of my childhood came up to my mind. I saw that wax doll as plainly as if I had it in my arms again. My brother Charles had taken a slate pencil and had made two cruel marks on its sweet face, and had left the house laughing at my rage and grief. All day long I had nursed my doll, rocking it back and forth in my arms and sobbing:

"Oh, my doll! Oh, my doll!"

Ada had said:

"Don't be silly. Dolls don't feel. But she is disfigured for life, like smallpox."

I threw her down. I rushed up to Charles' room, bent upon avenging her. Hanging on the wall was a lacrosse stick, the most treasured possession of my brother. I seized a pair of scissors and I cut the catgut of that lacrosse. As it snapped, I felt a pain and terror in my heart. I tried to mend it, but it was ruined.

Ada's shocked face showed at the door.

"I'm glad!" I cried to her defiantly.

"Poor Charles," said Ada, "saved up all of his little money to get that stick, and he did all those extra chores, and he's the captain of the Shamrock Lacrosse team. You are a mean, wicked girl, Marion."

"I tell you I'm glad!" I declared fiercely.

ONOTO WATANNA

But when Charles came home and saw it, he held that stick to his face and burst out crying, and Charles never, never cried. I felt like a murderer, and I cried out:

"Oh, I'm sorry, Charles. Here's all my pennies. You buy a new one."

"You devil!" he stormed and lifted up his hand to strike me. I fled behind papa's chair, but I wished, oh! how I wished, that Charles would forgive me.

It all came back to me like a dream, in the train, and I found myself crying for Charles even as I had cried then.

And again I began to think of Reggie, Reggie who had hurt me so terribly, Reggie whom I had thought I loved above everybody else in the world. What was it he had said to me? That I should be his wife without a ceremony! I sat up in the seat. I felt frozen stiff. I was looking at the naked truth in the plain light of day. The glamour was gone from my romance. I was awake to the bare, ugly facts.

The train was moving slowly, and some one said we were nearing Boston. I shook off all memories of Montreal and an expectant feeling of excitement came over me. What did this big United States mean to me? I felt suddenly light and happy and free! Free! That was a beautiful word that every one used in this "Land of the Free."

I went into the dressing-room and washed my face and hands and did my hair fresh. A girl was before the mirror, dabbing powder and rouge over her face, and she took up all the room so I could not get a glimpse of myself in the mirror.

"You look as fresh as a daisy," she said, turning around and looking at me, "and I guess you've had a good night's rest. I hardly sleep in those stuffy sleepers, and my fellow's to meet me so I don't want to look a fright."

I asked if we were near to Boston, and she said we were there now. The train had come to a standstill.

XXV

When I left the train with my bag in my hand, I felt excited and a little bit afraid. I realized that I had no special destination, and the part of the city where the station was did not look as if it was a place to find a room. There were many cars passing, and I finally got on one, a Columbus Avenue.

As we rode along I looked out of the window and watched the houses for a "Room to Let" sign, and presently we came to some tall stone houses, all very much alike, and ugly-and severe-looking after our pretty Montreal houses with their bits of lawn and sometimes even little gardens in front. There were "Room to Let" signs on nearly all the houses in this block. So I got out and went up the high steps of the one I thought looked the cleanest.

I rang the bell and a black woman opened the door. I said:

"Is your mistress in?" And she said: "How?"

We never say "How?" like that in Canada. If we aren't polite enough to say: "I beg your pardon," then we say: "What?" So I thought she meant, how many rooms did I want, and I said: "Just one, thank you."

She walked down the hall, and I heard her say to some one behind a curtain there:

"Say, Miss Darling, there's a girl at the door. I think she's a forriner. She sure talks and looks like no folks I knows."

There was a quiet laugh, and then a faded little woman in a faded little kimono came hurrying down the hall. I call her "faded-looking," because that describes her very well. Her face, once pretty, no doubt, made me think of a half-washed-out painting. Her hair was almost colorless, though I suppose it had once been dull brown. Now wisps of grayish hair stood out about her face as if ash had blown against it. She had dim, near-sighted eyes, and there was something pathetically worn-and tired-looking about her.

"Well? What is it you want?" she inquired.

I told her I wanted a little room, and said:

"I've just arrived from Montreal."

"Dear me!" she exclaimed, "you *must* be tired!" She seemed to think Montreal was as far away as Siberia.

She showed me up three flights of stairs to a tiny room in which was a folding bed. As I had never seen a folding bed before, she opened it up and showed me how it worked. When it was down there was scarcely an inch of room left and I had to put the one chair out into the hall.

She explained that it would be much better for me to have a folding bed, because when it was up I could use the room as a sitting-room and see my company there. I told her I did not expect any company as I was a perfect stranger in Boston. She laughed—that queer little bird-like laugh I had heard behind the curtain, and said:

"I'll take a bet you'll have all the company this room will hold soon."

There was something kindly about her tired face and when I asked her if I had to pay in advance—the room was three dollars a week—she hesitated, and then said:

"Well, it's the custom, but you can suit yourself. There's no hurry."

I sometimes think that nearly every one in the world has a story, and, if we only knew it, those nearest to us might surprise us with a history or romance of which we never dreamed. Take my little faded landlady. She was the last person in the world one would have imagined the heroine of a real romance, but perhaps her romance was too pitiful and tiny to be worth the telling. Nevertheless, when I heard it—from another lodger in the house—I felt drawn to poor Miss Darling. To the world she might seem a withered old maid. I knew she was capable of a great and unselfish passion.

She had come from Vermont to Boston, and had worked as a cashier in a down-town restaurant. She had slowly saved her money until she had a sufficient sum with which to buy this rooming-house, which I sometimes thought was as sad and faded as she.

While she was working so hard, she had fallen in love with a young medical student. He had even less money than Miss Darling. When she opened her rooming-house she took him in, and for three years she gave him rent free and supported him entirely, even buying his medical books, paying his tuition, his clothes and giving him pocket money. He had promised to marry her as soon as he passed, but within a few days after he became a doctor he married a wealthy girl who lived in Brookline and on whom he had been calling all the time he had been living with Miss Darling.

The lodger who told me about her said she never said a word to any one about it, but just began to fade away. She lost thirty pounds in a single month, but she was the "pluckiest little sport ever," said the lodger.

It seemed to me our stories were not unlike, and I wondered to myself whether Reggie was capable of being as base as was Miss Darling's lover.

While I was taking my things out of my suitcase, Miss Darling watched me with a rather curious expression, and suddenly she said:

"I don't know what you intend to do, but take my advice. Don't be too easy. If I were as young and pretty as you, I tell you, I would make every son of a gun pay me well."

I said:

"I'll be contented if I can just get work soon."

She looked at me with a queer, bitter little smile, and then she said:

"It doesn't pay to work. I've worked all my life."

Then she laughed bitterly, and went out suddenly, closing the door behind her.

As soon as I had washed and changed from my heavy Canadian coat to a little blue cloth suit I had made myself, I started out at once to look up the artist, Mr. Sands, whose address papa had given me.

I lost my way several times. I always got lost in Boston. The streets were like a maze, winding around and running off in every direction. I finally found the studio building on Boylston, and climbed up four flights of stairs. When I got to the top, I came to a door with a neat little visiting card with Mr. Sands' name upon it. I remembered that Count von Hatzfeldt had his card on the door like this, and for the first time I had an instinctive feeling that my own large japanned sign: "Miss Ascough, Artist," etc., was funny and provincial. Even papa had never put up such a sign, and when he first saw mine, he had laughed and then had run his hand absently through his hair and said he "supposed it was all right" for the kind of work I expected to do. Dear papa! He wouldn't have hurt my feelings for worlds. With what pride had I not shown him my sign and "studio!"

I knocked on Mr. Sands' door, and presently he himself opened it. At first he did not know me, but when I stammered:

"I'm—Miss Ascough. D-don't you remember me? I did some work for you in Montreal eight years ago, and you told me to come to Boston. Well—I've come!"

"Good Lord!" he exclaimed. "Did I ever tell anybody to come to Boston? Good Lord!" And he stood staring at me as if he still were unable to place me. Then after another pause, during which he stared at me curiously, he said:

"Come in, come in!"

While he was examining me, with his palette stuck on his thumb and a puzzled look on his face as if he didn't quite know what to say to me or to do with me, I looked about me.

It was a very luxurious studio, full of beautiful draperies and tapestries. I was surprised, as the bare stairs I had climbed and the outside of the building was most unbeautiful. Sitting on a raised platform was a very lovely girl, dressed in a Greek costume, but the face on the canvas of the easel was not a bit like hers.

Mr. Sands, as though he had all of a sudden really placed me in his mind, held out his hand and shook mine heartily, exclaiming:

"Oh, yes, yes, now I remember. Ascough's little girl. Well, well, and how is dear old Montreal? And your father, and his friend—what was his name? Mmmmum—let me see—that German artist—you remember him? He was crazy—a madman!"

Lorenz was the artist he meant. He was a great friend of my father's. Papa thought him a genius, but mama did not like him at all, because she said he used such blasphemous language and was a bad influence on papa. I remember I used to love to hear him shout and declaim and denounce all the shams in art and the church. He was a man of immense stature, with a huge head like Walt Whitman's. He used to come to the Château to see the Count, with whom he had long arguments and quarrels. He was German and the Count a Dane. He would shout excitedly at the Count and wave his arms, and the Count would shriek and double up with laughter sometimes, and Mr. Lorenz would shout: "Bravo! Bravo!"

They talked in German, and I couldn't understand them, but I think they were making fun of English and American art. And as for the Canadian—! The mere mention of Canadian art was enough to make the old Count and Lorenz explode.

Poor old Lorenz! He never made any money, and was awfully shabby. One day papa sent him to Reggie's office to try to sell a painting to the senior partner, who professed to be a connoisseur. Mr. Jones, the partner, came out from his private office in a hurry and, seeing Lorenz waiting, mistook him for a beggar. He put his hand in his pocket and gave Lorenz a dime. Then he passed out. Lorenz looked at the dime and said:

"Vell, it vill puy me two beers."

Reggie had told me about that. He was irritated at papa for sending Lorenz there, and he said he hoped he would not appear again.

I told Mr. Sands all about Lorenz and also about the Count I had worked for; about papa, some of whose work the Duke of Argyle had taken back to England with him, as representative of Canadian art (which it was not—papa had studied in France, and was an Englishman, not a Canadian), and of my own "studio." While I talked, Mr. Sands went on painting. The model watched me with, I thought, a very sad expression. Her dark eyes were as gentle and mournful as a Madonna's. She didn't look unlike our family, being dark and foreign-looking. She was French. Mr. Sands was painting her arms and hands on the figure on the canvas. He explained that the face belonged to the wife of Senator Chase. She was the leader of a very smart set in Brookline. He said the ladies who sat for their portraits usually got tired by the time their faces were finished, and he used models for the figures, and especially the hands.

"The average woman," said Mr. Sands, "has extreme ugly hands. The hands of Miss St. Denis, as you see, are beautiful—the most beautiful hands in America."

I was standing by him at the easel, watching him paint, and I asked him if it were really a portrait, for the picture looked more like a Grecian dancing figure. Mr. Sands smiled and said:

"That's the secret of my success, child. I never paint portraits as portraits. I dress my sitters in fancy costumes and paint them as some character. There is Mrs. Olivet. Her husband is a wholesale grocer. I am going to paint her as Carmen. This spirituelle figure with the filmy veil about her is Mrs. Ash Browning, a dead-and-alive, wishy-washy individual; but, as you see, her 'beauty' lends itself peculiarly to the nymph she there represents."

I was so much interested in listening to him, and watching him work, that I had forgotten what I had come to see him about, till presently he said:

"So you are going to join the classes at the Academy?"

That question recalled me, and I said hastily:

"I hope so, by-and-by. First, though, I shall have to get some work to do."

He stopped painting and stared at me, with his palette in his hand, and as he had looked at me when he opened the door.

I unwrapped the package I had brought along with me, and showed him the piano scarf I had painted as a sample, a landscape I had copied from one of papa's and some miniatures I had painted on celluloid. I said:

"People won't be able to tell the difference from ivory when they are framed, and I can do them very quickly, as I can trace them from a photograph underneath, do you see?"

His eyes bulged and he stared at me harder than ever. I also showed him some charcoal sketches I had done from casts, and a little painting of our kitten playing on the table. He picked this up and looked at it, and then set it down, muttering something I thought was: "Not so bad." After a moment, he picked it up again and then stared at me a moment and said:

"I think you have some talent, and you have come to the right place to *study*."

"And work, Mr. Sands," I said. "I've come here to earn my living. Can you give me some painting to do?"

He put down his palette and nodded to Miss St. Clair to rest. Then he took hold of my hand and said:

"Now, Miss Ascough, I am going to give you some good advice, chiefly because you are from my old Montreal (Mr. Sands was a Canadian), because of your father and our friend, good old man Lorenz. Finally, because I think it is my duty. Now, young lady, take my advice. If your parents can afford to pay your expenses here, stay and go to the art schools. *But* if you expect to make a living by your painting in Boston, take the next train and go home!"

"I can't go home!" I cried. "Oh, I'm sure you must be mistaken. Lots of women earn their livings as artists. Why shouldn't I? I worked for Count von Hatzfeldt, and he said I had more talent than the average woman who paints."

"How much did he pay you?" demanded Mr. Sands.

"Five dollars a week and sometimes extra," I said.

Mr. Sands laughed.

"You would starve on that here even if you could make it, which I doubt. In Montreal you had your home and friends. It's a different matter here altogether."

I felt as I once did when, as a child, I climbed to the top of a cherry tree, and Charles had taken away the ladder, and I tried to climb down without it. I kept repeating desperately:

"I won't go back! I tell you, I won't! No, no, nothing will induce me to go back!"

I gathered up all my paintings. I felt distracted and friendless. Mr. Sands had returned to his painting and he seemed to have forgotten me. I saw the model watching me, and she leaned over and said something in a whisper to Mr. Sands. He put his palette down again and said:

"Come, Miss St. Denis. This will do for to-day. We all need a bit of refreshment. Miss Ascough looks tired."

I was, and hungry, too. I had had no lunch, for I lost so much time looking for Mr. Sands' studio.

He brought out a bottle wrapped in a napkin, and a big plate of cakes. He said:

"I want you to taste my own special brand of champagne cocktail."

He talked a great deal then about brands of wines and mixtures, etc., while I munched on the cakes which I found difficulty in swallowing, because of the lump in my throat. But I was determined not to break down before them, and I even drank some of the cocktail he had mixed for me. Presently, I said:

"Well, I guess I'll go," and I gathered up my things. Mr. Sands stood up and put his hands on my shoulders. Miss St. Denis was standing at his elbow, and she watched me all the time he was speaking.

"Now, Miss Ascough, I am going to make a suggestion to you. I see you are determined not to go back. Now the only way I can think of your making a living is by posing."

I drew back from him.

"I am an artist," I said, "and the daughter of an artist."

He patted me on the back.

"That's all right. I know how you feel. I've been a Canadian myself; but there's no use getting mad with me for merely trying to help you. You will starve here in Boston, and I'm simply pointing out to you a method of earning your living. There's no disgrace connected with such work, if it is done in the proper spirit. As far as that goes, many of the art students are earning extra money to help pay their tuition that way. The models here get pretty good pay. Thirty-five cents an hour for costume posing and fifty cents for the nude. We here in Boston pay better than they do in New York, and we treat them better, too. Of course, there are not so many of us here and we haven't as much work, but a model can make a fair living, isn't that so, Miss St. Denis?"

She nodded slowly, her eyes still on me; but there was something warm and pitying in their dark depths.

"Now," went on Mr. Sands, "I don't doubt that you will get plenty of work. You are an exceedingly pretty girl. I don't need to tell you that, for, of course, you know it. What's more, I'll safely bet that you have just the figure we find hard to get. A perfect nude is not so easy as people seem to think—one whose figure is still young. Most models don't take care of themselves and it's the hardest thing to find a model with firm breasts. They all sag, the result of wearing corsets. So we are forced to use one model for the figure, another for the legs, another for the bust—and so on, before we get a perfect figure, and when we get through, as you may guess, it's a patchwork affair at best. Your figure, I can see, is young and—er—has life—*esprit*. Are you eighteen yet?"

"I'm nearly twenty-two."

"You don't look it. Um! The hands are all right—fine!—and the feet"—he smiled as I shrank under his gaze—"they seem very little. Small feet are not always shapely, but I dare say yours are. Your hair—and your coloring—Yes, I think you will do famously. It's rather late in the season—but I dare say you'll get something. Now, what do you say? Give over this notion of painting for a while, and perhaps I can get you some work right away."

"I'll never, never, never pose—nude," I said.

"Hm! Well, well—of course, that's what we need most. It's easy to get costume models—many of our women friends even pose at that. However, now would you consider it very *infra dig.* then to pose for me, say to-morrow, in this Spanish scarf. You are just the type I need, and I believe I can help you with some of the other artists."

I thought of the few dollars I had left. I had only about twelve dollars in all. Mr. Sands said he would pay me the regular rate, though I was not experienced. After a moment's thought I said:

"Yes, I'll do it."

"Now, that's talking sensibly," he said, smiling, "and Miss St. Denis here will take you with her to other places to see about getting work."

She said:

"Yes, certainement, I will do so. You come wiz me now."

I thanked Mr. Sands, and he patted me on the shoulder and told me not to worry. He said he would give me some work regularly till about the middle of May when he went away for the summer. I would get thirty-five cents an hour, and pose two hours a day for him.

When we got to the street, the lights were all lit and the city looked very big to me. Miss St. Denis invited me to have dinner with her. She knew a place where they served a dinner for twenty-five cents. She seemed to think that quite cheap. I told her I couldn't afford to pay that much every night and she said:

"Well you will do so by-and-by. Soon you will get ze work—especially eef you pose in ze nude."

I said:

"I will never do that."

She shrugged. After dinner she took me to a night school where she posed, as she said she wished me to see how it was done. Of course, I had already seen Lil Markey pose for the Count, but she was just an amateur model then. It did seem worse to me, moreover, to go out there before a whole class than before one man. Miss St. Denis seemed surprised when I said that, and she declared it was quite the other way.

That night I sat in my little narrow bedroom and looked out of the window, and I thought of all I had learned that day, and it seemed clear to me that Mr. Sands was right. There was little chance of my making a living as an artist in Boston. What was to become of me then? Should I return home? The thought of doing that made me clinch my hands passionately together and cry to myself:

"No, no; never, never!"

I remembered something Mr. Davis had said to me when he was teaching me to act. He said that I should forget my own personality and try to imagine myself the person I was playing. Why should I not do this as a model? I resolved to try it. It could not be so bad, since Mr. Sands had recommended it. Yes, I would do it! I would be a model! But I should not tell them at home. They would not understand, and I did not want to disgrace them.

With the resolve came first a sense of calmness, and then suddenly a rush of rage against Reggie who had driven me to this. I had the small town English girl's foolish contempt for a work I really had no reason for despising. As the daughter of an artist, and, as I thought, an artist myself, it seemed to me, I was signing the death warrant of my best ambitions and, as I have said, I felt, with rage, that Reggie was to blame for this. I looked out of that window, and lifting up my eyes and clasped hands to the skies, I called:

"O God in heaven! hear me, and if ever I go back to Reggie, curse me, and may all kinds of ills come upon me. Amen!"

Now, I thought, as I got into that folding bed, "I don't dare to go back, for God will curse me if I do."

ONOTO WATANNA

XXVI

My trunk arrived next morning, and the driver charged me fifty cents to bring it from the station. I had always seen Reggie tip the drivers, so I offered him a nickel. The driver was a big, good-natured looking fellow, and he looked at the tip and then at the little room, and he said:

"I'll not take the tip, kid, but I'll be catching you around the corner some evening and take a kiss instead."

He had such a merry twinkle in his eye and looked so kind that somehow I didn't resent his familiarity. I even vengefully laughed to myself, to think how Reggie would have looked to hear that common man speak to me like that.

All of that day I went with Miss St. Denis to the studios and schools, waiting for her in some of them while she posed, and stopping only for a few minutes in others while she introduced me. I got several engagements and Miss St. Denis made me jot them down in a notebook she brought along. She said I must take everything offered to me, but that I must be careful not to get my hours mixed. I should even work at night, if necessary, for the season was almost over, and soon I would have difficulty in getting any engagements unless I was willing to pose nude at the summer schools. Nearly all the artists went away in summer—at least the ones who could afford to pay for models—and she predicted a hard time for me, unless I changed my mind about the nude posing.

I liked Miss St. Denis, and I respected her, too, even though she did seem to have no shame about stripping herself and going right out before whole classes of men.

Miss Darling had told me about a boarding place opposite her house, where I could get good board for three dollars a week. I crossed over that evening and entered one of those basement dining-rooms that lined almost the whole avenue. I had a newspaper with me, and while I waited for my dinner I went over the advertisements.

I was interrupted by a stir and movement in the room. A girl had come in with a little dog, and everybody was looking at the dog. She came over to my table and took the seat directly in front of me. I stared at her. I could not believe my eyes. There, sitting right at my table, was my little sister, Nora! I had thought she was in Jamaica.

We both jumped to our feet and screamed our names, and then I began to cry, and Nora said hastily: "Sh! They are all looking at us!"

The dining-room was full of medical students and Harvard students. I had noticed them when I came in—one reason why I buried myself in the paper, because they all looked at me, and one, a boy named Jimmy Odell (I got to know Jimmy well later) tried to catch my eye, and when I did look at him once, he winked at me, which made me very angry, and I hadn't looked up once again, till Nora came in.

You may be sure those students didn't take their eyes off us all through that meal, and every one of them fed Nora's dog. They had started to laugh and hurrah when Nora and I first grabbed at each other, but when I cried they all stopped and pretended to fuss with the dog.

I don't know what I ate that day. Nora said I ate my meal mixed with salt tears, but she, too, was excited and we both talked together. Nora had changed. She seemed more sophisticated than when I saw her last, and she had her hair done up. She showed me this almost the first thing, and she said it made her look as old as I. She thought that fine. She assumed an older-sister way with me which was very funny, for I had always snubbed her at home as being a "kid" while I was a grown-up young lady.

When we went to her room, which, strange to say, was in the same block as mine, two of the students followed us, one of them that Odell. We didn't pay any attention to them, though Odell had the insolence to run up the steps when Nora was turning the key in the lock, and ask if he couldn't do it for her. We both regarded him haughtily, which made him ashamed, I suppose, for he lifted his hat and ran down the stairs again.

Nora's room was just about the same as mine, only she had a narrow cot instead of a folding bed, and she had a box for her foolish little dog. He was a white fox terrier and was not very good, for if she left him a single moment you could hear his cries all over the neighborhood. Consequently she was obliged to take him with her whenever she went out. I was awfully provoked next day, because I wanted her to go with me to the studios, but that miserable little dog made such a fuss that she turned back before we had reached the corner. She said she'd bring him along. I told her she was crazy. No girl could go looking for work with a dog along. She seemed to prefer the dog to me, which made me much huffed with her, for she went back to her room.

Nora was expecting money by telegraph from some doctor in Richmond, for whom she was going to work. She had been doing the same sort of work as Ada, writing for a newspaper, and she had written "tons of poetry and stories and other things," she said.

I wanted to talk over home things, and the work we were to do, etc., but Nora made me listen to all her stories. She would pile up the two pillows on her bed for a comfortable place for me, and then coax me to lie there while she read. She would say:

"Now, Marion, let me make you comfortable, and you rest yourself— you look awfully tired, and I'm sure you need a rest!—while I read you this."

Then she would read one story after another, till I would get dead tired, but if I closed my eyes she would get offended; so I'd hold them open no matter how sleepy I got. Sometimes I couldn't help laughing at the funny parts in her stories, which delighted her, and she would laugh more than I would, which would make her little dog yelp and jump about. Then when I cried in sad parts, she would get much excited, and say:

"Now I know it must be good. Some day huge audiences in big theatres all over the world will be crying just as you are now."

Then her dog would jump up and lick her face, and I would say:

"Don't you think that's enough for to-night?"

Poor little Nora! She had hardly any money, but it didn't seem to bother her a bit. Though I knew I would miss her, I advised her to take the steady position offered in Richmond, instead of starving here, and a few days later I saw her off for the South. She looked pathetic and awfully childish (in spite of her hair done up), and I felt more lonely than ever. I was crying when I got back to the lodging-house, and when I opened the door, Miss Darling was standing talking to some man in the hall. She called to me just as I was going up the stairs:

"Miss Ascough, here's a nice young gentleman wants to meet you."

I came back down the stairs, and there was that Harvard student, Odell. He had a wide smile on his face, and his hand held out. There was something so friendly and winning in that smile, and somehow the pressure of his big hand on mine felt so warm and comforting, and I was so lonely, that when he asked me to go out with him to dinner and after that to the theatre I said at once:

"Yes, I will."

Thus began my acquaintance with a boy who devoted himself to me throughout his stay in Boston, and who, in his way, really loved me.

XXVII

I had been posing for various artists for nearly two months, and I not only was used to the work but beginning to like it. How else, except as a model, could I have seen all I did at close range, and, in a way, assisted in the making of many great paintings by the best artists in Boston? Also I learned much from them, for nearly every artist I posed for talked to me as he worked. Some would tell me their hopes and fears and stories about other artists. I have even been the confidante of their love affairs.

One well-known painter proposed to a girl upon my advice. He told me all about his acquaintance with her, and of the opposition of her family as if he were telling a story, and then he asked:

"What would you do if you were the man in the case?"

I replied:

"I'd go right over and ask her to-night." Whereupon he picked up his hat and said:

"I'll do better than that. I'll go this minute."

One artist, famous for his paintings of sunlight, used to talk all the time he worked, and I realized that he was not talking to me but at me, for when I answered him he didn't hear at all.

I didn't make, of course, more than a living posing in costume, but for a time I got about four hours' work a day. It was not always regular, and sometimes I didn't even get that much time. Then there were days when I had no work at all, so I barely made enough to pay for my room and board. I realized that I would have to do something to increase my earnings, and I tried to get work to do at night schools. Miss St. Denis had told me there would be little chance there unless I would pose in the nude, and that I was determined not to do, but as the summer approached my work grew less and less, for the artists began to go away just as Miss St. Denis had told me they would.

Though Mr. Sands had said I was an exceedingly pretty girl, I found that beauty was by no means an exceptional possession, and especially among the models. There were much prettier girls than I, to say nothing of the many girl friends and relatives of the artists who were often willing to pose for them. So my good looks did not prove as profitable as I had hoped. Moreover, I was new at the work, had an acquaintance to build up, and at first tired quicker than the older models.

However, I made a number of good friends among the artists. One of them, dear old Mr. Rintoul, who had a studio in that long row of studios near the art gallery. One day, I knocked at his door and applied for work as a model. He opened the door and peered out at me in the dark hall. At first he said he was sorry, but he couldn't use me. He was a landscape-painter, and he said he guessed I had come to the wrong man, as there was another artist of his name on Tremont Street who painted figures. Then he said:

"But come in, come in!"

He was a little man of about fifty, and his face had the chubby look of a child. He wore the funniest old-fashioned clothes. He peered up at me through his glasses, and seemed to be examining my face. After a moment he said:

"Having a hard time, eh? Or are you extra busy now?"

I told him I was not extra busy, and he rubbed his chin in a funny way and said:

"I believe I can use you after all. Now I'll tell you how we'll arrange it. I'm a pretty busy man, so I can't make any definite engagement, but you come here whenever you have nothing else to do, and I'll use you if I can. If I'm too busy, I'll pay you just the same. How will that do?"

I thanked him, and told him I was so glad, for work was getting scarcer every day.

He pointed to a big armchair and said:

"Now sit down there and rest yourself. Be placid! Be placid!" He waved his hand at me, and went to see who was knocking at the door. Then he came back and said:

"Too busy to use you to-day. Here's the money," and he handed me seventy cents, as if for two hours' work.

"Oh, Mr. Rintoul," I said, "I haven't worked at all."

"Now don't argue," he said. "That was our agreement, so be placid!"

One day when I went to pose, he said that all the people in the studios were giving a tea, and they had asked him to open the doors of his studio, so the visitors could see it. He remarked that he would take that day off. I said:

"There must be an awful lot of artists here."

He chuckled, and making his hand into a claw, said:

"Not all artists, but folks hanging on to the edge of art, and cackling, *cackling*! Now run along, and keep placid!" and he handed me a dollar for my "time."

I never really posed for him at all, for he always had something else to do, but he would make me sit in the big armchair and "be placid."

He is now gone to the land where all is placid, and whenever I hear that word I think of him, and my faith in good men is strengthened.

But not all of my experiences with the artists of Boston were as pleasant as that with Mr. Rintoul and Mr. Sands and some others. I had one terrible experience from which I barely escaped with my life.

I had posed several times for a Mr. Parker, who did a rushing business for strictly commercial firms. He made advertisements such as are seen on street-cars, packages of breakfast food and things like that. I had posed for him in a number of positions, to show off a certain brand of stockings as a girl playing golf, to advertise a sweater, and other things too numerous to mention.

He was a large, powerfully built man, devoted to sports, and he used to tell me about his place at Cape Cod, and how he fished and rode. He discovered that I could paint, and he let me help him sometimes with his work. We got to be very friendly, and I really enjoyed working for him and liked him very much. His wife was a sweet-faced gentle little woman who occasionally came to the studio, and she would sometimes put an extra piece of cake in his lunch box for me. He said she was a saint.

Of all the artists I worked for my best hopes rested on Mr. Parker, for he had promised, if certain work he expected came, he might be able to employ me permanently—not merely as a model, but assisting him.

One day after I had been working for him all morning, and we had lunch together, I sat down on a couch to glance over a book of reproductions, when I felt him come up beside me. He stood there, without saying anything for a while, and then, stooping down, brushed my cheek with his beard. I was not quite sure whether he was leaning over to look at the pictures, but I did not like his face so close, and half-teasingly I put up my hand and pushed his face away, as I might a fly that was in my way. Suddenly I felt a stinging slap on my face. Surprised and angry, I leaped to my feet.

"Mr. Parker, you are a little too rough!" I said. "That really hurt me."

I thought he was joking, but when I saw his face I realized that I was looking at a madman.

"I intended to hurt you," he said in the strangest voice, and then he cursed me and struck me again on the cheek with the flat of his

ONOTO WATANNA

powerful hand. "Take that, and that, and that!" His voice rose with each blow. Then he took me by the shoulders and shook me till my breath was gone.

"Now I'm going to kill you!" he raved.

I fell down on my knees, and screamed that I had not meant to offend him, but he caught hold of my hands and dragged me along toward the window, shouting that he was going to throw me out. We were seven stories up and he had dragged me literally on to the window sill. I tried to brace myself for death, as all my resistance seemed as nothing to his awful strength; but even while we struggled at the window, the door of his studio opened and some one came in. Like a flash he turned, and dragging me across the room, he literally threw me into the hall and shut the door in my face. To this day I do not even know who had entered his studio, but I believe it was a woman, and sometimes I wonder if it could have been his wife.

In the hall I gathered myself up. My clothes were nearly torn off my back, and I was black and blue all over. My hair was down, and blood was running down my chin. I climbed upstairs to the studio of another artist I had posed for, and when he opened the door to my knock, he was so startled by my appearance that he called to his wife, a sculptress, to come quickly.

"What is the matter? Whatever is the matter?" she asked, drawing me in. "You poor girl, what has happened to you?"

I could not speak at first. I tried to, but my breath was coming in gasps, and I was sobbing. For the first time in my life hysterics seized me. They chafed my hands and brought me something to drink, and then she held my hands firmly in hers, and bade me tell her what had happened. Between sobs, I described the treatment I had received. I saw husband and wife exchange glances, and I ended:

"And now I'm going to have him arrested."

"Listen to me," said Mrs. Wilson. "I know you have suffered terribly, and that man ought to be killed; but take my advice, keep away from the police. Remember you have no witnesses. You could not prove the assault. It would be your word against his and you are only a model. Let it pass, and hereafter keep away from Mr. Parker."

Her husband said:

"I'm surprised at Parker, the damned brute! I've heard of queer doings down there, and I knew he had beaten messenger boys, but, by Jove, I didn't dream he'd beat a girl. You must have aroused his temper in some way. You know he's unbalanced—of course you know that—every one does."

No, I did not know that. He was worse than unbalanced, however. He was a madman.

I went home bruised and sore and, as they advised, let the matter drop. As Mrs. Wilson had said, I had no witnesses, and I was just a model!

XXVIII

It was the second week in May, but as warm as summer and the flowers were all blooming in the parks. The artists were leaving Boston early that year. There seemed only a handful of them left in town. I had scarcely any engagements. Mr. Sands had left, and so had four other artists for whom I had been posing. Mr. Rintoul, too, had gone away. I could no longer go to Mr. Parker, the man who had beaten me.

I sat in my little hall room, reading a letter from home.

Dear Marion: (wrote Ada)
    We are all very glad to hear you are doing so well in Boston" (I had told them so) "and we hope you will come home this summer.
    Papa is not at all well and mama awfully worried. There is not much money coming in. I am doing all I can to help, and I gave up a good position offered me by the C. P. R. to travel over their Western lines and write travel pamphlets, because I will not leave mama just now.
    Charles would do more, but his wife won't let him. I think you ought to help. Ellen has been sending money regularly, but now Wallace is ill. Even Nora sends something each week.
    I must say, Marion, that you always were the one to think only of yourself, and you always managed to have a good time. Now as you are earning money in the States, and there are so many younger ones at home, you certainly ought to send home some money. It is wicked of you not to.
    You will be sorry to hear that Daisy (the sister next to Nellie) went into the convent to be a nun last week. She simply was bent upon it and nothing we could say or do would stop her. You know she became a convert to the Catholic faith soon after Nellie married de Rochefort. She is with the Order of the Little Sisters of Jesus, and her name is now Sister Marie Anastasia. We all feel very badly about it, as she is so young to shut herself up for life.
    Last Sunday I went for a walk as far as the Convent of Les Petites Sœurs de Jesus, and I looked over the garden

fence, but I could see no sign of our Daisy. So I called: 'Daisy! Daisy!' and oh, Marion, I felt awful to think of her behind those stone walls, just like a prisoner, and I even imagined I saw her face looking out of one of the windows of the solemn, ghostly-looking convent building. It is a very hard Order. We did everything to dissuade her, but one night she took the pilgrimage to Ste. Anne de Beaupré on a sort of prayer ship, and she never got off her knees all night long. Do you remember what beautiful hair Daisy had—the only one in our family with golden hair—well, it is all shaved off, mama says, though that was unnecessary till her final vows. So we've lost Daisy. It's just as if she were dead.

Have you broken off your engagement to that Reggie Bertie? You know I always said he was no good, and I never believed he really loved you. That kind of man only loves himself. Anyway there is no need to get married if you can earn your own living. I think most men are hateful.

I met that Lil Markey on the street and she asked for your address. She said she was going to New York. She's pretty common, and if I were you I'd not associate with her. You should have some pride.

Write soon, and send some money when you do. Sooner the better. Love from all,

Your aff. sister,
Ada

I looked at my money. I counted all that I possessed. I had just six dollars and twenty cents. I was badly in need of clothes, and I was only eating one meal a day. For breakfast and lunch I had simply crackers. Still, I felt that those at home probably needed money more than I did. So I wrote to Ada:

Dear Ada
I was so sorry to hear papa is ill, and that you were all having a hard time; so I enclose $4, all I can spare just now. I am not making as much as I thought I was going to when I last wrote you; but I'll soon be doing fine, so don't worry about me, and tell papa and mama everything is all right.

It's awful about Daisy. She's a poor little fool, and yet perhaps she is happier than any of us. Anyway I guess she feels peaceful. It must be sweet not to have to worry at all. Still I don't believe in any stupid churches now.

You don't understand about Reggie. He was and is in love with me, so there, and he writes to me every day begging me to return. I guess I know my own affairs better than you do. I have no more news, so will say good-bye, and with love to all,

Your aff. sister,
MARION

I posted my letter and then started out to keep an engagement to pose for an illustrator on Huntington Avenue. He had a charming studio apartment in a new building. I knew both Mr. Snow and his wife pretty well, for I had posed for most of his later work. They had only been married a little while. She was very pretty, and sweet, too. He was a tall, rather lanky man of about thirty, and his long teeth stuck out in front under his mustache. He made a great deal of money, as he said he had the knack of making pretty girls' faces, and that was what the magazines wanted.

He told me one day that there was a time when he had not known where his next meal would come from. Then he had met his wife. He said: "Her family are the Reynolds of Cambridge, and they had the dough all right." She had really started him on the way to success.

He was in a very genial mood that afternoon, and chatted away while he drew my head. He was making a cover for a popular magazine. I had removed my waist, and arranged some drapery about my shoulders to give the effect of an evening gown.

When he was through, and I was buttoning up my waist in the back, he came behind me and said:

"Allow me," and started to button my waist for me, but while he was doing it, he kissed me on the back of my neck.

"I think—" I began, when a sweet voice called from the doorway:

"I have brought Miss Ascough and you some tea, dear."

Mrs. Snow had entered the room, carrying a tray in her hand. She was a frail, pretty little thing, with beautiful reddish hair piled on top of her head. Mr. Snow went forward and took the tray from her hands, and, bending down, he kissed the hands holding it.

"Thank you, darling," he murmured. "What an angel you are!"

She looked at him with such love and trust in her eyes that I decided no tale of mine should hurt her. I made up my mind, however, not to pose for Mr. Snow again. So there was another of my artists gone! I left that house wondering if it were possible to believe in any man, and then I thought of Mr. Rintoul and I felt warmed and comforted.

XXIX

It was getting dark as I walked down Huntington Avenue and somebody was walking rapidly behind me, as if to catch up with me.

"Hallo, Marion!"

I turned, to see Jimmy Odell. He had been hanging around my lodging-house for days, and was always coaxing me to go to places with him and declaring that he was in love with me.

I liked Jimmy, though the people where I took my meals told me he was no good. They said his people had given him every advantage, but that Jimmy had played all his life and that his mother had spoiled him. However, I found him a most lovable boy, despite his slangy speech and pretended toughness of character. Jimmy liked to pretend that he was a pretty bold, bad man of the world. He was in his junior year at Harvard and about my own age.

Many a time when it seemed as if I could not stand my life, I was cheered by Jimmy with his happy, contagious laughter, and the little "treats" he would give me. Sometimes it was a ball game, sometimes a show and I had had many dinners and suppers with Jimmy. But Jimmy drank far too much. He didn't get exactly drunk, but he carried a flask of whiskey with him, and he would say to whoever was about:

"Have a drink," and if no one accepted he would say: "Well, here's to you, anyway," and drink himself.

It was no use my lecturing him about it, for he would just laugh at me and say:

"All right, grandma, I'll be good," and then go right ahead and do it again.

Once when he told me for the hundredth time that he loved me and begged:

"Come along. Let's get married and fool 'em all."

I said:

"If you do without whiskey for two weeks, and then come and tell me on your honor that you have not touched it, maybe I will."

He said:

"That's a go. I take you up!" and we shook hands solemnly on it; but the very next time he came to see me, I smelled the whiskey on him, and he said he hadn't started the "two weeks' water-wagon stunt" yet.

I was glad to see Jimmy's happy face that evening, and, tucking my hand in his arm, we walked along the avenue.

"Gee!" said Jimmy, as we passed the hotels all lighted up and looking so inviting and fine, "I wish I had the cash to blow you to a wine supper, Marion, but, I seem to spend every d——cent before I get it."

"Never mind, Jimmy," I said. "I've my meal ticket for that boarding-house."

"Oh, that hash-slinging joint!" groaned Jimmy. "Say, Marion, I know a dandy place on Boylston Street, corner of Tremont, where there is mighty good grub and beer, and they don't soak a fellow fancy prices. Let's go there now, what do you say?"

"All right, but I thought you said you were broke?"

"Oh, that's all right," he replied airily. "Come along, and don't ask questions."

Somehow when I was with Jimmy, I never felt serious and I seemed to catch his happy-go-lucky spirit and say to myself: "Oh, well, I don't care!"

Gaily we started for Jimmy's restaurant. We had reached Elliott Street, when Jimmy said:

"Hold on a minute. You wait in this doorway for me a moment, Marion. I have to see a man on a matter of business."

I stepped into the doorway, but I watched Jimmy. He swung into a shop over which there were hung three golden balls. Oh! I knew that place for I had already visited it. It sheltered my engagement ring—the ring Reggie had given to me! In a few minutes out came Jimmy minus his spring overcoat. It is true the day had been warm, but the nights were still chilly, and I felt badly to see him without his coat.

"Jimmy, what have you done? Where's your coat?"

"Oh, that's all right," he laughed. "I just left it with my uncle over night. My mother won't give me a red cent when I ask her—thinks I ought to eat at home or beat it for the country, now college's closed—but she gives it to me all right—with tears, Marion—when she sees me next day without my coat. So come along."

My feelings were mingled. If I did not go with him, I knew he would spend it all on drink. Besides, he had pawned his coat for me, and I felt it would be ungrateful to refuse to go with him now.

Jimmy ordered us a splendid supper, oysters, a big steak, beer; but it would have tasted better if I had not known about that overcoat, and I almost cried when we got out to the street, and he had to turn the collar of his coat up.

XXX

The following night Jimmy turned up sure enough, not only with his overcoat, but, as he said, "the price of another bang-out."

He said his mother had wept when she saw him "shivering," and "you better believe no one ever shivered better than I did," said Jimmy.

So I went to supper again with Jimmy. When we were sitting at the table, and he started to order beer for me, I said:

"Now, look here, Jimmy, I'll eat supper with you, but I won't drink with you, and that's all there is to it."

"Be a sport, Marion."

"I don't pretend to be a sport," I replied, "and anyway in Montreal that means to shoot or skate or snowshoe or toboggan. Here when you say 'sport' you mean to drink a lot of liquor. I think it's horrid."

Jimmy regarded me reproachfully.

"I bet those farmers in Montreal drink their share all right," he said. "Of course, that bum Canadian village isn't really on the map at all" (he was teasing me), "but I'll bet the booze is right there. Say, don't you really have cars running there? I bet you had some fine Jay-farmer beaus all right—oh! How about the one whose letters you're always so glad to get? You nearly fell down the stairs the other day in your hurry to get that one from Miss Darling."

I couldn't help laughing to think of Reggie being called a farmer. Jimmy took offense at my laughing.

"Say, what're you laughing about anyhow? If you don't want my company, say so, and I'll take myself off."

"Don't be silly, Jimmy. You know very well I like your company, or I wouldn't be sitting with you now."

"Then why can't you drink a glass of beer with a fellow? I bet you would if I were that Montreal chap."

"I'll drink the beer on one condition," I said. "If you'll promise not to drink any whiskey to-night."

Jimmy leaned over the table.

"I'll promise you anything on earth, Marion. I'm half-crazy about you anyhow."

The waiter was passing, and looking at us, he said:

"No kissing allowed."

Jimmy was on his feet.

"What the devil do you mean? Did you mean to insult this lady?"

His voice was raised and he had seized that waiter by the collar. I felt ashamed and afraid. I jumped up and tried to pull Jimmy from the waiter, but he wouldn't let go.

"Please, Jimmy, for my sake, stop!" I pleaded. The waiter was smiling a forced sort of smile, and he said:

"No insult was intended, sir."

"All right then, apologize to this lady."

The waiter did so.

"And now," said Jimmy in a very lordly way, "come along, Marion, we don't have to stay in this place. Come along."

When we got out to the street I turned upon him and said:

"You can take me home, Jimmy Odell. I won't go into another restaurant with you. I'm not going to be disgraced again."

"Oh, all right-oh!" said he sulkily. "I guess I can get all the whiskey I want alone without any one preaching to me," and he turned around as if to leave me. I ran after him and caught him by the arm.

"Jimmy, don't drink any more."

He tried to shake off my hand, and he said recklessly:

"What difference does it make? You don't care anything about me. You wouldn't really care if I drank myself to death."

"I would care, Jimmy. I care an awful lot about you."

Jimmy stopped short in the street.

"Do you mean that? You do care for me?" I nodded. "Very well, then," said he, "it's up to you to stop me. If you'll marry me, I'll quit the booze. That's on the level, Marion."

"Now, Jimmy, you know what I told you before, and yet you couldn't keep away from that old flask of whiskey. You love it better than me. And I'm not going to marry you till I *do* see some real signs in you of reforming. Besides, anyway, you've got two years still to finish at Harvard, and I guess your people would be crazy if you got married before you graduated."

"Say, who is marrying, they or me?" demanded Jimmy. "Ah, come along, like a good fellow. Here's just the joint we want," and he drew me into a chop house on Washington Street.

No sooner was he seated at the table than he ordered two steins of beer for us, but he kept his word about the whiskey. I had difficulty in drinking from the stein, as the lid knocked my hat crooked, and this amused Jimmy vastly. He began to chuckle loudly all of a sudden, and he leaned over the table and said:

"Tell you what I'll do, Marion. My sister's giving some sort of party to-morrow night. How'd you like to go along?"

"Why, how can I? She hasn't invited me."

"Well, I guess I can bring *my* friends to our house if I want," declared Jimmy, as though some one had questioned his right. "Will you or won't you go? Yes or no?"

"We-el—"

"No 'well' about it. Yes or no?"

"Yes."

XXXI

I didn't have any work at all to do the next day, so I stayed in and fixed up a pretty dress to wear to the party at Jimmy's house. He called early for me, bringing along another student named Evans, who played the guitar. We stopped for Benevenuto, an Italian, who played the mandolin with Evans, and whom I had met several times.

At the last moment, I hesitated about going and I said:

"Maybe your mother and sister won't want me. If they knew I was a model, I'm sure they wouldn't."

"Great Scott!" burst from Jimmy, "that just proves how beautiful you are, Marion. If I were a girl, I'd be proud to say the artists wanted me for all those fine paintings. I've not seen a magazine cover to compare with your face, Marion, and, say—my folks ought to be proud to know you, eh, Evans?"

Evans grinned, and Benevenuto nodded violently. It was nice to have Jimmy think so well of my "profession," and I didn't tell him that all models were not necessarily beautiful. Some of them are very ugly but "paintable."

As we were going along in the car, Jimmy said to Evans:

"Say, Bill, you want to get next to my sister's friend, Miss Underwood. She's a fine girl, and has heaps of dough. My sister wants her for a sister-in-law, but little Jimmy has his own ideas." Turning to me, he added with a tender smile: "She can't begin to hold a candle to you, Marion."

Jimmy's people lived in a very fine house, and I felt much impressed and somewhat anxious as we passed in. His sister looked like Jimmy and had his features, but where the tall, swinging figure and handsome features made a fine-looking man, the same type in a woman did not make a beauty. She looked hard and bony. Her manner to me was of the most frigid, and I saw her give Jimmy an angry glance, as he airily presented me. She kept him on one excuse or another right by her side and that of a very tall girl all evening. Benevenuto and Evans were soon playing for the company, and I, who had not been introduced to many of the people, found a quiet corner of the room, where I could sit unobserved and watch every one.

I had been there some time, and Benny and Evans had given way to a girl who was singing in a high voice "The Rosary," when I heard Benevenuto's voice speaking softly in my ear:

"Miss Marion, will you me permit to call upon you?"

He was small and dark, and his hands were soft and brown. He had shining black eyes and hair that curled. He could play beautifully, the reason why the students at the boarding-house chummed with him; and then Evans was a great favorite with them all, and the two were indispensable to each other. They got engagements to play together in concerts and musicales. Evans was working his way through college in this way. Many people looked upon Benevenuto as a musical prodigy. He could play almost any musical instrument. His father was a barber, his brother a cook; but all of his humble relatives were contributing to the musical education of this talented member of their family.

I had never given Benny much thought or attention, except when he played in the room below me, where Evans roomed. I would open my door and listen to the strains of music, and sometimes Evans would call up to me to come down. One day I had been listening to them play, and when they got through joked with Benny about something. He came over and sat down beside me on the couch, and he said:

"I like-a you, Miss Marion. You look like my countrywomen."

Miss Darling had said to me that night:

"Be careful how you flirt with an Italian. They are pretty dangerous fire to play with."

So when that night of the party, Benevenuto asked me if he might call, I thought of that, and I said:

"Oh, I'll see you when you are playing in Mr. Evans' room some night."

"No," he persisted. "I like-a make special call on you. Please to permit."

To humor him, I said:

"Oh, all right, and bring your mandolin."

He smiled at me ecstatically and said fervently:

"Me—I am coming right away to-morrow night."

It was time to go. Most of the guests were going into the bedroom for their wraps. Nobody noticed me. So I slipped into the room where Jimmy had taken me upon my arrival there. It was his mother's, he had said, but she was away at their country place. I noticed on the bed a black straw hat with a steel buckle holding the severe bit of plumage, and I thought to myself that it was probably his mother's hat, for no one else had put their wraps in this room. I was putting on my own hat at the mirror when I heard some one say:

"Sh-h!"

I turned around, and there was Jimmy in the doorway. He was whispering with his hand to his mouth.

"Marion, say good-night to my sister quickly, and then sneak away. I'll be waiting on the porch."

So I found my way back to where his sister and a number of guests were, and I wished them good-night and thanked Miss Odell for the lovely time I had not had.

"Good-night," she returned coldly, "your friend, Mr. Benevenuto, will see you home." Then she turned to the girl at her side: "Jimmy will be delighted to take you home, dear. He is still in the supper-room."

I felt like saying:

"He is waiting for me!"

As we walked home, Jimmy said:

"I couldn't get away from sis. Gad! that friend of hers may be handsome, but I hate handsome horses. I like a little pony like you, Marion."

"Don't you think I'm handsome then?" I asked mischievously.

"Not by a long shot. You are the most kissable—little—"

"Jimmy, behave yourself. Look at that policeman watching us, and don't forget that waiter."

"Oh, hang policemen and waiters," growled Jimmy. "What the devil do *they* know about kisses?"

"When you want to kiss me, Jimmy Odell," I said, "you'll have to come without that whiskey odor on your breath."

"Oh, all right-oh!" said Jimmy. "I guess there are others won't mind it."

"No, I guess not," I sniffed. "Horses haven't much smelling sense."

ONOTO WATANNA

XXXII

There was a rap on my door. I opened it, and there was Benevenuto. He had on a black suit. It looked like the suits the poor French Canadians dress their dead in. He had plastered his hair so sleekly that it shone like a piece of black satin, and oh! he did smell of barber's soap and perfume. His big black eyes were shining and he was smiling all over his face.

"Where is your mandolin?" I asked.

"I have called to see *you*," he answered. "Me, I am not musician to-night." Then as he saw my evident disappointment, he said, "but if I am not welcome for myself, I can go."

I felt really sorry for him, as his smiling face had become so suddenly mournful and stormy-looking. So I said:

"Oh, I'm really glad to see you," and I tried to smile as if I were. He came up to me with a kind of rush and said excitedly:

"Marion, I love-a you! I love-a you! I love-a you! Give me the smile again. That smile is like music to me. I love-a you!"

I was amazed and also alarmed.

"Mr. Benevenuto," I said, backing away from him, "please go away."

I thought of what Miss Darling had said, that Italian men were not to be played with. I had merely smiled at Benny, with what a volcanic result! He was coming nearer and nearer to me, and he kept talking all the time, in his soft, pleading way:

"Marion, I have love-a you from the first day I have look at you. You look-a like my countrywomen, Marion. We will getta married. Soon I will make plenty money. We will have maybe little house and little bebby."

I could stand it no longer. He was only a boy after all, and somehow he made me think of the little beggar boy I had pinched when I gave him the bread and sugar. I pushed him away from me, and I said:

"Don't talk such foolishness. I am old enough to be your mother." I think I was about three years older than he.

"No matter, Marion," he said, "no matter. I do not care if you are so old. I love-a you just same."

I was sidling round along the wall, and now I had reached the door. I ran down the stairs, and I did not stop till I reached the safety of Miss Darling's room.

"What on earth is the matter?" she cried, as I burst in.

Between laughter and tears I repeated the interview. She couldn't help laughing at me, especially when I told about the part of "the little bebby." Then she said:

"Well, we'll get him out now, but you must never, never flirt with an Italian. You're apt to be killed if you do."

Later in the evening Jimmy came. He was very quiet and queer for Jimmy, and he sat down on my window sill, and held his head in his hands. When I told him about Benevenuto, he looked up and said:

"The damn' little rat. I'll throw him out of the window."

After a moment he said:

"Come over here, Marion, I want to tell you something."

I sat down on the opposite side of the window seat.

"Say, Marion, there's a hell of a row going on up at my house about you. Sis kicked up an awful fuss, and they're all on to my coming to see you. Sis declared I insulted her friend, because I took you home instead, and mother is mad, too. They make me sick. Mother asked me where your folks lived, and what you were living alone like this for, and they insinuated some nasty things. Lord! women have rotten minds. I told them that you were a hard little worker, and then they wanted to know what you did, and I told them you were a model, and that I was proud of it. But, gosh! you ought to have heard those women! When I told them that, they almost burst themselves mouthing about it. I turned on 'em and told them not one of them could be a model. They didn't have the looks. But the long and short of it is that mother has telegraphed for dad, and she says she won't give me another cent unless I promise to give you up. As I needed a ten-spot I said I would, but you better believe I'm not going to do it."

I stood up and put my hand on Jimmy's shoulder. Somehow I felt older than Jimmy, though we were about of an age. He seemed such a boy, so wayward and reckless, and there was so much that was lovable about him, despite his "toughness."

"Jimmy dear," I said, "I guess your mother's right. You'd better give me up. It'll only make trouble for you if you keep on coming to see me."

"Tell you what I'll do," said Jimmy. "I'll quit college, and get a job of some sort. Then I'll be independent, and I'll come to see you all I damn' please, and I'm going to marry you whether they want me to or not."

I thought of Jimmy's happy-go-lucky nature and his love of drink, and I determined the poor fellow should not lose the help of his family if I could avoid it. We took a little walk around the block, I urging Jimmy all the time to please do what his people wished, and I even told him that while I was fond of him I did not love him. He said savagely that he guessed I had left my heart in Montreal, and then he pulled his cap down over his eyes, and didn't say anything for a long time. We just tramped around, and then Jimmy said suddenly:

"Say, Marion, why doesn't he come on here and marry you if he loves you? Is it lack of money prevents him?"

I said:

"*I* don't want to marry *him*. That's the reason why." How I wished that was the truth!

"Well, say, girlie, let's you and I get married on the Q. T. Then I'll go West, as they're talking of shunting me out there, and as soon as I've made good you can join me. How's that for a scheme?"

"It sounds pretty nice, Jimmy, but I'd rather do the marrying *after* you've made good."

"Oh, it'll be dead easy," declared Jimmy. "I've an uncle out there with a ranch as big as a whole county. It'll just be like dropping into a soft snap, don't you see?"

I sighed.

"'Making good' isn't merely dropping into soft snaps, Jimmy," I said sadly.

Jimmy suddenly whistled under his breath, and I saw him looking at a couple of women who were coming toward us. He raised his hat as they passed us, but although the younger woman returned his bow, the older one stared at him indignantly, and then she gave me a very severe and condemning glance. All of a sudden I knew who that woman was. I recognized her by her hat. She was Jimmy's mother!

The following day, I had a letter from her. She said I was ruining her son's future, and if I did not give him up he would soon be without a home. She said that he was in serious trouble with his father, and that the latter intended to send him out West, and that she hoped I would do nothing to prevent her son from going. Finally she said that if her son were to marry a model the family would never forgive him and that such a disgrace would break all of their hearts, besides ruining him.

I did not answer her letter. I sat for a very long time thinking about my life. What was there wrong about being a model, then, that society should have cast the bar sinister upon it? Surely, there was no disgrace in one who had beauty having that beauty transferred to canvas. I had long ago ceased to despise the profession myself. The more I posed, the more I felt even a sort of pride in my work, though I still thought one was "beyond the pale" when one posed completely nude.

Miss Darling knocked at my door, and brought in a telegram. I thought at first it was from Reggie—that he was at last coming, as he had been threatening in all of his letters to do, and my hands were trembling when I broke the flap. But it was from poor Jimmy—Jimmy en route to Colorado, entreating me to write to him and assuring me that he never would forget his "own little Marion," and that he would "make good" and I'd be proud of him yet. I sat down to write an impulsive answer to the boy, and then my eye fell upon his mother's letter. No! I would not ruin her son's life. Jimmy should have his opportunity, but I said to myself with a sob:

"And if Jimmy ever does make good, they'll have *me* to thank for it, even if I am an artist's model!"

XXXIII

June had come and I was filling the last of my engagements. There was not a single other day on my calendar for the week, and it was Wednesday. I had had only two engagements the week before.

I was posing for three women. The work was easy, as they were amateurs, and liked to meet together and use the same model, and paint and have a social time. I was posing in a gypsy costume, and they talked to me occasionally in a patronizing way, as if I were a little poodle. One of them asked me if I wouldn't like to paint. I knew I could paint better than she could, but I pretended to simper and said:

"Oh, yes, indeed."

One of the women, with kind-looking eyes, smiled at me and asked me if I managed to make a living, and then the one who had asked me if I would like to paint said:

"Oh, by the way, we won't need you again, as we are all off for the country."

She added that they might be able to use me the next season, and I wondered dully to myself whether I would need them when the new season came. A feeling of despair was stealing over me—despair and recklessness.

The woman with the kind eyes who asked me if I made a living, I have since recognized as the wife of the President. I wish I had known her better.

Though I had so little work to do, nevertheless I was feeling languid and tired in these days, and when I reached my room that afternoon, I threw myself bodily down upon my bed. I felt that I did not want to get up even to go out for my dinner. I was lying there with my face buried in the pillow, when Miss Darling called up the stairs:

"There's a gentleman to see you, Miss Marion."

I jumped up and ran out into the hall. A short, dark man was mounting the stairs. I thought at first he was a picture-dealer I had once seen at Mr. Sands' studio.

"Miss Ascough?" he asked.

I bowed and led him to my room.

He said he had obtained my name from Mr. Sands and that he wanted to engage me as a model for some decorative work he was doing. He had seen me several times about the studio buildings, and had decided I was the type for this particular work. As he said the work would last all summer, I was delighted, and I thanked him fervently. Then he said:

"Suppose we have a little supper together somewhere."

I was awfully sorry, but I had promised to help Miss St. Denis fix a waist she was making. So I told this man I could not disappoint my friend. He said: "As you please then," and was going, when I asked him for his address. He stopped and thought a moment, and then he wrote something on a slip of paper and handed it to me. He told me to come to work at ten the following morning, and, bowing, went. The address was in Brookline, and as it was some distance out I planned to start early to be sure to be there on time.

After the man had gone, all my lassitude vanished. I felt like dancing and screaming, I was so relieved and happy. Here I was engaged for six hours' work a day for all of the summer. I rushed over to tell the good news to Rose St. Denis. She said:

"I think it is too good to be true. It looks too easy. I think he will want the model to pose nude, ha? You will not do so yet?" As I shook my head, she said with a nod: "You will make very poor living if you don't do so, mon enfant. The artists have not enough to keep one model in work in the costume, and then there are so many doing the same thing. Every girl—all ze actress and ze chorus girl—even ze frien' of ze artists, she will pose in ze costume. Ze model cannot get enough work to keep her, unless she is friend of some one or, maybe, she is complaisante to ze artist—yes. Only when she pose nude in ze schools—see—she get ze work, so long as she have ze belle figure. It is so. Now, which a model prefer? Pose in nude, starve—or perhaps be maitresse to somebody— which is ze same thing," she added with a shrug as "aller au diable!" (to go to the devil!)

"Which would you prefer?" I asked her.

"Mon dieu! some funny question you ask," said the French girl. "It is because I love my Alfred (Alfred was her fiancé) that I pose nude for ze other mens; for because I pose comme ça I can keep myself good and pure for only him. It would be more easy if I were not good. Do you not see, enfant? I pose and stand on my poor feet for three, four, and sometimes nine heures a day—nine heures when I do night work, and for zat I get me fifty cent one heure. The bad girl she get very liddle time more moneys than I; but me? I keep me my respect. Yes—it is so. Soon

ONOTO WATANNA

my Alfred, he will come from France and we will marry. Then, enfant, ah! we will be happy like cheeldren."

Somehow when she was speaking, this model who posed in the nude, she looked like the Virgin Mary, and I put my arms around her and kissed her. She said:

"Pauvre enfant! Me? I know eet is hard for you! I have ze pity for you; but dat will not put ze food in ze stomach! Non! Soon you will see!"

Happily I awoke next morning. I was going to start at good, steady work. Now, I thought, I would pay Lu Frazer back all I owed her, and I'd send mama some money every week, and Reggie's letters should go unanswered. He had written me saying that he was coming soon to Boston to bring me home, unless I returned myself. And, I thought, I would buy myself a new hat, and trim it with violets.

I went into the basement dining-room to get my breakfast, and the landlady put a bill at my plate. It was for three dollars for meals I had had. I told her I would pay her sure in a few days.

I had exactly five cents in my pocketbook when I started for Brookline, but I intended to ask the artist to pay me a little in advance. They often did that, and as I was to have steady work, I was sure he would not object. I could not help thinking of a remark of my father's, that something always "turned up" and I felt that my something had come in the nick of time.

It was three-quarters of an hour's ride to the street in Brookline he had marked on the card. I got off at last, and walked down the street, looking at the numbers. I went up and down twice, but I could find no such address. I went to nearly every second house on the street, but no one knew the name I inquired for, and the clerk in the drug store where I also inquired said there was no such man in the vicinity. Again and again I looked, and then a sick sense of apprehension stole over me, and I began to realize that I was the victim of some beastly hoax.

What in heaven's name was I to do? I had no carfare even, and it was too far to walk. I wandered about distractedly, and then I finally resolved to get on the car, and when the conductor should ask for my fare, I would pretend I had lost it. Then, I thought, "even if he puts me off, I will be that much nearer home, and I will try another car."

So I got on a car, but I suffered the shame of a cheat, when the conductor finally came up to me, and I almost cried as I pretended to search through my empty pocketbook. Then I heard the conductor's voice. He was a big red-faced Irishman, with freckles on his face, and he grinned down at me:

"Aw, dat's all right, kid!" he said, and taking a nickel from his own pocket, he rang up my fare. When I was getting off, I said:

"Thank you, I'll send it back to you, if you give me your name."

He laughed:

"Dat's all right, kid," he said, and then leaning to my ear, he added: "Say, do you want another nickel, sissy?"

XXXIV

I borrowed a dollar from Evans, the student who was a friend of Jimmy's. I bought the morning papers, and scanned the columns of advertisements. I was determined to look for some other kind of work, yet I realized that I was a "Jack of all trades and master of none," unless it be that of the model. I found one advertisement that seemed to be pretty good:

"WANTED: A smart, pretty young lady for light, easy work. Experience not necessary."

I started down town to answer that advertisement at once. The address was in the old building Washington Street, and there seemed to be all kinds of business carried on there. On the door of the place I was to apply was some name, and the word "Massage." I had a dim idea what massage meant. I associated it in some way in my mind with illness. I pushed the bell, and the door was quickly opened. A stout, matronly woman stood smiling at me.

"Come in, dearie," she said, as though she were expecting me.

I found myself in a room that looked like the average boarding-house parlor. It was stuffy and dark. The woman set herself down in a rocker, and she was still smiling at me.

"I came in answer to the advertisement. What do you require me to do?"

Patting me on the arm, she said:

"Easy, easy, dear. Don't talk so loud. It is massage work, dearie."

"I can't do it," I said, "but I might be able to learn."

She kept on grinning and winking at me, and I don't know why, I suddenly felt terribly afraid of her. I said tremulously:

"Will I have to wear aprons?"

She got out of the rocking chair and poked me in the side.

"Now, dearie, if you are really a good girl, I don't want you to come at all. I rather have a young married lady. I had a sweet little married lady before, but her husband got on to us and—"

I had begun to back toward the door, and with my hand behind me, I found the knob. I ran out into the hall, and down those stairs as quickly as I could get. Oh, how good the air did seem, when I found myself at last on the street.

When I got back to my room, I found a note on my table. It was from Miss Darling, and was as follows:

DEAR MISS MARION

I don't want to press you, but could you let me have the rent? I would not bother you, but I have expenses to meet, and even if you could let me have a part of it if you cannot let me have it all, I would be obliged.

C. DARLING

There was a letter, too, from Reggie. I opened it with my hatpin, and, oh! I think if I could have pierced Reggie instead of that letter just then I would have liked to do it.

DARLING GIRLIE

I met your sister Ada on the street, and she tells me you are doing awfully well in Boston with your painting. I hope, however, you are not forgetting your old sweetheart. Ada tells me you are coming home this summer. Darling, I shall try to arrange to go to Boston, and we will come back to Montreal together. I am longing for the moment when I can hold my own little Marion in my arms again, and tell her how much I love her.

Everything's going my way lately, and you'll see me a Q. C. before many years have passed.

Your own,
REGGIE

Somehow I blamed Reggie for all I had suffered and as I stared out at the darkening night descending upon the streets, I muttered to myself:

"Now it is your fault that I am compelled to pose nude."

It had come to this at last. There was nothing else for me to do, and Miss Darling must be paid. She had been so good to me.

As I went out I knocked at Miss Darling's door. She put out her head and I said:

"Dear Miss Darling, it's all right. I'm going to pay you in a few days."

She said: "All right, dear, I know you will keep your word."

Yes, I would keep my word! I was on my way to Miss St. Denis to tell her what I was now willing to do. I found her in, but she was not feeling well. She had been posing at a class the previous night, she told me, and also three hours in the afternoon.

"See my feet," she said, thrusting them out, "Mon dieu! they are so sick. All ze night I have put me some vaseline and it is no good. They are all grown so beeg again."

Her poor, bare feet were badly swollen. I begged her to let me bathe them in hot water. Mama always bathed our feet in hot water when we had colds or our feet hurt.

"Bien!" she said. "Do so, enfant, if you wish, but it is so hard to get hot water in dese boarding-houses. Ah! very soon I will have dat little house of all my own, and den, you will see, enfant, what it is to be très happy!"

She sighed, as if she were inexpressibly tired, and lay there with her dark eyes closed, and her beautiful soft, dark hair all about her lovely oval face, and I thought to myself again: "She looks like a picture of the Virgin," and I felt sure that although she was just a poor model, she was pure and good like the Virgin. She opened her eyes after a moment and smiled at me, and she said:

"When I have my little house, enfant, then always ze water will be hot. There will be ze gas on ze stove, and it will give beeg flame. I will have plenty for heat my water. Here, me, I stand and hold for eternity ze little pot to make some water hot on ze little gas jet. It is all stuff up full!" and she closed her eyes again.

"Wait a minute," I said. "I'll go and ask your landlady for hot water."

I found my way down to the basement, and very politely I said to the landlady:

"Miss St. Denis has a very bad foot. Will you be so kind to let me have a pitcher of hot water?"

She snapped back at me:

"I guess I give my roomers more hot water than they pay for. Does she think she is paying hotel prices?"

In a begrudging manner, she poured me out half a pitcherful from the kettle on the range. Thanking her, I started to carry it up, but a loose piece of carpet at the foot of the stairs caught my feet. I slipped, and all my precious hot water was lost. The landlady had picked up the pitcher, which fortunately was not broken, and when she saw me crying, she began to laugh uproariously, and seemed to be suddenly good-natured, for she refilled the pitcher.

I bathed Rose St. Denis' feet, and made her comfortable, and she thanked me very sweetly and seemed to be grateful. I sat beside her bed for a while, smoothing her forehead. She was not really ill, just tired out. Presently I said:

"Now the time has come for me to pose nude, too, or as you say, starve or go to the devil."

She opened her eyes with a start, and she said:

"Dieu! But you say things so suddenly, enfant. You are funniest girl. You say sometime ze ting I would not dare to speak, for if I did I would have to confess to my priest; and den you are so afraid to do some tings dat is nuttings wrong, and you mek one beeg fuss for dat."

She sat up in the bed, with her knees drawn up, and regarded me with the benignant tolerant glance of a wise young mother. She could understand my viewpoint in regard to posing nude, but she believed I was simply wrong and my stubbornness in the matter had always puzzled her. She did not waste any time on pitying me now. On the contrary she urged me to do the work.

"Now you have come," she said, "at a very good time, for me. I am not able to go to dat night class, and I have made engagement for all of dis week. You will take my place, voilà! First you will go to ze master of ze school, and you will tell him you have pose bi-fore, dat you have ze belle figure—yes, you must say dat. If necessaire you will show him." As I shook my head, she nodded at me and said: "Yes, yes, you will do dat, if necessaire. Mebbe he will not require. You must not tell him dat you have not pose bi-fore in dat altogedder. He will tink you 'greenhorn,' as you say, den. Tell him you are one professional model, and dat you are frien' to Rose St. Denis, and dat you will tek my place. I tink he will be satisfy. You look liddle bit like me—like you are liddle sister to me. Yes, dat is so."

She patted my hand, smiling comfortingly at me. Then she went on with her instructions. It was only Tuesday, and I would have five evenings' work and earn seven dollars and fifty cents. I would probably also be engaged for the following week, and for the day classes of the summer school. A model as much in demand as was Rose St. Denis sometimes got steady work of nine hours a day. Three in the morning, three in the afternoon, and three at night. She assured me that I would be soon as much in demand as she was, perhaps more so, since I was younger than she.

The seven dollars and fifty cents I felt would be a godsend at this time. I would be able to pay the boarding-house woman. She had stopped me on the street only that morning and said:

"If you don't pay me, Miss Ascough, you will have no good luck."

Then there was Miss Darling. I must keep my word to her. Moreover, Ada had been writing me urgent letters insisting that I should send something home, for Wallace, Ellen's husband, was very ill, and, of course, no help was coming from them now. As I looked at Miss St. Denis, I thought to myself that after all it could not be such dreadful work, or she would not do it. She seemed to me the embodiment of sweetness and refinement, and I could not imagine her doing anything that was gross or impure. I remembered that even the time I saw her posing nude before the class, I had not felt revolted in the way I had that time when Lil Markey had skipped about the Count's studio. The amateur model, Lil, had been simply brazen. The professional one was seriously doing her honest duty. There were many other girls in Boston I had met who were doing the same work, and most of them were good girls. Mr. Sands had said that modesty and virtue did not always go hand in hand, and that it was his experience that some of the most immoral women appeared to be the most modest and shy.

Miss St. Denis was lying back again among her pillows, with her white hands—the hands Mr. Sands had said were the most beautiful in America—clasped at the back of her head. She was watching me, and I suppose she knew I was turning the matter over in my mind, and I do not doubt but what she realized somewhat of the struggle that was wrestling in my heart. After a while she said:

"Enfant, pass me dat bottle on ze dresser."

I did so, and she pressed it back into my hand.

"See," she said, "it is ze spirit dat will give you courage. I will give it to you. The moment dat you all undress yourself, tek one good long drink, and den, enfant, you will forget dat you have no clothes on your body, and dat tout le monde, he is look at you—your feet, your legs, your stomach, and every piece of you dat you do not like them to see. It will be joost like little dream. Dat firs' time, also, I am feel ze shame—but soon it pass—and it is all forget. Courage, enfant!"

"No, no, Miss St. Denis. Oh, I can't do it! I can't!" I began to cry, and then she seized hold of my hands fiercely and pulled herself up in bed.

"Ah, you are ze coward—renegade! You will not help me."

"Oh, Miss St. Denis, I might just as well go to the devil completely. Oh, I can never, never do it! Oh, if my people found out, I would be eternally disgraced and Reggie—he would never speak to me again.

Then, surely, he would *never*, never marry me, and there would go my last hope."

"You are hystérique," she said gently. "I t'ink you have not eat so much—yes?"

I told her I had had my dinner, which was not true, and after a while, when I had dried my tears and was feeling more composed, she resumed, just as if I had not said I would not do it.

"It is not so hard as you t'ink. You will yourself undress behind ze screen dat they provide, wiz one chair for you to rest upon. Nobody look at you when you take off dose clothes. Dere also is one wrapper for you to cover over your body, and when ze monitor he call: 'Pose!' you will walk wiz ze wrapper on top you to ze model stage, and only den you will drop ze wrapper. Listen, enfant! If you have take dat dreenk I am tell you 'bout, you will forget dat it is your body, and dat you have on no clothes. You will say to yourself: 'Dis is not me. Dis is jus' some statue—so many lines for dem to draw and paint, to make some peecture. Ze real me, I am lef' in my clothes dat are behind dat screen. Voilà, enfant?"

I was beginning to get her spirit, and I said:

"Why, yes, I do see. It's like acting, isn't it? I *will* forget it is I." I tried to laugh and added: "I will say: 'O Lord, have mercy on me, this is none of me!' That's an old Mother Goose rhyme, Miss St. Denis." Because I could see she had fatigued herself on my account, and it was my turn now to comfort and reassure her, I put my arms about her and hugged and kissed her. Tears came into my eyes, and she murmured:

"Pauvre petite enfant! You look like ma petite sœur!"

XXXV

I went directly from Miss St. Denis' to the school. I asked to speak to Mr. Lawton, the master, and he came out to the little anteroom and looked at me sharply while I spoke. I knew my voice was trembling but I said as bravely as I could:

"I have come from Miss St. Denis. She is ill; but I will take her place."

"You have posed nude before?" he asked, his eye seeming to scan me from head to foot.

"I am a professional model," I answered.

"Hm! Yes, I think you will do."

I was behind the screen. I had taken off all of my clothes, and I was wrapped up in the wrapper which I found to be very dirty. I wondered how many girls had wrapped it about them.

I could hear the students entering the class-room. I peeped out, and already there were about fifteen men of various ages, and there were about thirty easels and stools. More students were coming in. There was one elderly man with white hair, and two young boys, one only about thirteen. He looked like my little brother, Randle. I began to redress. I could never go out before those men and the little boy! Merciful God, no!

Then I remembered my promise to Miss Darling. I thought of my father, who was ill, of Ada's insistent demands, of my empty pocketbook, and then I thought of the bottle that Miss St. Denis had given to me. I undressed again. I heard a voice saying:

"Where's the model?"

Then the voice of the monitor called sharply: "Pose! Pose, please!"

I drained that bottle dry. I stepped from behind that screen. I walked up to the platform, and I flung off the wrapper. I heard a voice saying, as from a distance:

"Stand a little to the left." I obeyed.

"Take some poses," said the voice. I obeyed.

I stood there immovable. I felt like a slave who was to be burned as an offering by some savages. It seemed as if I were turning to stone. There was a vague ringing in my ears, and then, as Miss St. Denis had foretold, I forgot that class. I did not see it. I was back in Hochelaga, and Charles was dragging me along on a sleigh. The snow was thick on our clothes. Mama was brushing it off. Charles was pulling off his mittens, and I heard him say to mama—as, oh! he had said a hundred years ago, it seemed—"Mama, I'll never take that Marion with me again. When we pass the Catholic store with all those images of saints, she makes me so ashamed. She will stop to look at the naked Jesuses. I couldn't make her come away."

"Rest! Rest!"

The voice of the monitor! I awoke. Mechanically I pulled the wrapper over me. Somebody said:

"The model is crying."

I walked behind the screen. My head still swam, and I still saw dim visions of my home. I seemed to have been there only five seconds—it was five minutes—when again came the command:

"Pose!"

Now I felt angry. I stepped on that stage again, and once more I threw off the wrapper. Somebody said:

"Put the left foot further back."

My anger was mounting. The dream had all vanished and I was conscious only of a vague fury. I know not why, but, oh! I hated all of those men. They were looking at me, I thought, like cruel tormentors. I wanted to hurt them all, as they were hurting me. Their intent looks, some with their eyes narrowed to see better, others measuring me with a plumb string, seemed to be mocking at my pain. Somebody said:

"She looks cross."

I seized the wrapper and savagely I wrapped it about me. I ran for the screen, shouting:

"Oh! you devils! You beasts! You shall not torment me any more."

Again I was behind the screen, and with mad, hurrying, fumbling hands I was dressing myself. There was the scraping of boots and stools, and several whistles from the class-room, after that first silence.

Then the master came behind the screen.

"What does this mean, Miss Ascough?" he demanded. I was crying bitterly. "Did anyone say or do anything to offend you? If so, I'll put him out of the class."

I said:

"Oh, yes, they are not gentlemen. They all stared at me and talked about me."

There was an indignant murmur of denials from the students. Mr. Lawton put his head over the screen and I saw him wink to the students. Then he turned to me and said in a coaxing voice:

"Now, now, be a good girl. We want you to finish the pose. If anybody dares to be rude to you, you just tell me about it, and I'll put him out."

"No, no," I said. "I'll not do it again."

"Now please, won't you for my sake? It's instruction night, and I am here to give criticisms.

Please resume the pose like a good girl. Yours is just the kind of figure we need. Come, now."

"No—no—I am through forever!"

I was all dressed. Oh, my beloved clothes! Never again would I remove them.

The teacher was now thoroughly provoked.

"What do you mean by taking an engagement and wasting our time like this?"

"I don't know," I answered, and I ran out of the room.

I owe an apology to that class.

XXXVI

We were all sitting around the big hall stove, and papa said:

"Put your feet on the fender, Marion, and get them warm."

Mama was feeding me with a big spoon of ice-cream, which Reggie tried to snatch away, and then he would throw red-hot coals in my face. Screaming:

"Reggie! Reggie! Stop! Stop!" I woke up.

A man was sitting on the bed in my little room, and he was holding my wrist. I recognized him as a young doctor who had attended Miss Darling when she had the grippe. He had straight blond hair and a gentle expression. Standing by him was the girl who had taken the big room on the first floor a few days before. I had noticed her, because she dressed so well and had so many visitors. Now she was holding some ice on my head, and I heard her say to the doctor that she had just put a hot-water bag on my feet. She was not beautiful like Rose St. Denis, for she was short and stout, but she had a large, generous mouth, which, when she laughed, showed the most beautiful teeth, and she laughed a great deal so that one could not help liking her. "How is she, doctor?" she asked, and he replied:

"She ought to stay in bed some time. Her temperature is a hundred and five. I'm afraid of her being left alone. Has she no one to take care of her?"

"No, no," I moaned weakly. "I have nobody. They are all dead."

"Who was that 'Reggie' you were calling for?" asked the girl, and I said:

"He's dead, too."

My eyes felt very heavy, and I could not keep them open. I heard their voices as if in a dream.

"My! but she gave us a scare," said the girl. "We were just going out of the front door last night to get a bite of supper over at the Plaza, and as we opened the door she was coming up the front steps, and she suddenly threw out her hands as if she were drowning, and would have fallen down the stairs had not Al caught her."

There was a long silence, and then I heard her voice again—she was stroking my hand.

"Poor girl! What a *pretty* little thing she is."

I put my cheek against her hand. Somehow it seemed to me natural that she should be good and kind to me. Then the doctor said:

"I will have her moved to the hospital. This room is too small, and she will need the best of care."

"Why can't I care for her?" asked the girl suddenly. "I can do it! Oh, you don't believe me, eh?" I heard them both laugh, and she said:

"It'll be lots of fun. To begin with, you carry her down to my room."

"Do you really mean that?" I heard him ask, and her reply: "Why, of course, I do."

I did not say a word. I did not care much what they did to me, and there seemed to me no reason why I should not be cared for by this stranger. I suppose it was my weakness, but perhaps it was the consciousness that I would have done the same in her place. Poor girls instinctively depend upon each other in crises like these. And then this girl—Lois Barret was her name—had a jolly way that made even the most trying service seem like a game to her. She acted as if she really enjoyed doing something that another person would have considered a trial. She kept saying:

"It'll be all kinds of fun. Come along, doctor, let's get her right down now. Can you do it?"

"Easily," declared the doctor.

"Ah!" said she. "It's fine to have big, broad shoulders. I wish I were a man—like you." She added the last two words softly, and the doctor chuckled. They wrapped the blankets around me, and the doctor lifted me up in his arms and carried me down the stairs. I was so weak, that even this slight movement affected me, and I fainted.

I must have been even iller than the doctor thought, for I did not know anything more for a long time. Then one day I opened my heavy eyes, to find myself in a big sunny room, and dreamily I watched Lois Barret hovering over me like a ministering angel. Then, in the evening, I have a dim remembrance of the doctor standing in the window and putting his arm around Lois, and it seemed to me he was kissing her. I called out:

"Oh, I am not asleep. I can see you."

They both laughed, and Lois came over and gave me something to swallow and, as I dropped asleep, they seemed to grow into one person.

XXXVII

L ois, are you in love with Doctor Squires?" She burst out laughing.

"I'm in love with everybody and everything. Here, lie back there."

I was to sit up in bed that afternoon, and the following day in a chair. I had been ill two weeks.

"Now," said Lois, "I have to go down town on some business, and I'll be gone two hours. If you want anything just knock on the wall with this," giving me a brush, "and Billy Boyd in the next room will come in, and if it's something he can't do himself, he'll call Miss Darling."

She kissed me, and, looking fresh and radiant, she went out.

Billy Boyd roomed with a friend in the next room to Lois. His roommate was a clerk in a department store, and Billy was a cable operator. He worked at night. Reggie would have called these boys "common Yankees." I knew how much better, and in every way superior, they were to Reggie, whose grandfather was a Duke of something or other. These boys would run errands for Lois if she knocked on their wall for help, and when I was most sick and helpless Billy even came in and helped Lois when it was necessary to lift me. Lois treated them as if they were girls, and they treated her as if she was a boy. It was a revelation to me, as in Canada, as in Europe, the simple friendship between men and women is not known as in the United States.

Then there was big Tim O'Leary. He was a bartender in a nearby hotel. He had a room in the basement of what had once been the dining-room. He used to knock at the door and ask in his big voice, which sounded for all the world like a foghorn:

"How's the little Canadian girl?"

He would send the waiters from the hotel where he worked over with all sorts of stuff that a sick person was not allowed to eat, big platters of lobster salads, chicken salads, club sandwiches, wine and beer. Lois told him I could only have a little broth, and then Tim sent over a big pitcher of rich soup. Lois tasted it, and then fed a spoonful of it to the doctor, and they both laughed. Then she went to the boys' room and knocked, and they were glad to get the good stuff.

Tim was a man of immense stature, and he would tell us all kinds of stories of his experiences when he was a coalheaver in New York and the fights he got into, and the times he was arrested, and always got off with a light fine. Dr. Squires called him a "rough diamond," and, much-sought-after society man as Doctor Squires was, he liked to go off with Tim O'Leary and have a drink and "chin" together. I did admire the doctor for that, and I remembered how Reggie had been ashamed and angry with me because I had spoken to the conductor on the train, who had been an old schoolmate of mine.

There was a knock at the door, and I called "Come in." The door was cautiously and softly opened, and Tim thrust in an inquiring face.

"How's yourself?" he inquired in a big whisper.

"I'm very well, thank you, Mr. O'Leary," I said.

"And Miss Barret, how's herself?"

"Oh, she's well, too. She had to go out for a couple of hours."

"Sure then I'll stay and take care of you mesilf," said Tim. "I'm dead tired. Standing behind a bar is hard on the feet; so if you don't mind, I'll be taking off my shoes and stretch mesilf out on the couch for a rest."

I assured him I would be very glad to have him do it. The big man worked sometimes ten and twelve hours at a stretch, and it was so quiet and peaceful in this room, I felt the rest would do him good, just as it was doing me.

XXXVIII

The sun was shining and the warm breath of summer felt good to me. I was up now; but I felt impatient with my own weakness and I had a restless desire to move about and do things. I realized my indebtedness to Lois, and I wondered if I would ever be able to wipe it out.

I had had very dreadful news from my people. Wallace, Ellen's husband, had died after a long illness. When I first heard that I wanted to go at once to my sister, and I was heart-broken because of my inability to comfort and help her. Lois wrote to Ellen for me, telling her that I would join her in New York, just as soon as I was strong enough to travel; but Ellen had written back that she was going to England with her little boy to Wallace's people.

I thought of how close Ellen and I had been to each other as children, and of the strangeness and cruelty of fate that cut sisters apart. It seemed to me that this was a world of all pain. Yet, if we measured our griefs by those of others, mine shrank into insignificance beside those of Ellen. Always there had been some way out for me, but Ellen's road had been walled up. Death had shut to her forever the golden door of Hope. I knew that no one—not even her little son—could ever take to Ellen the place of Wallace, her young hero and lover and husband. Poor Wallace! Literary critics had said he was a genius, and I think that he was. He was only twenty-seven when he died, with his second book of essays but half written and his play still unproduced.

Lois had a little gas stove in the room on which she boiled coffee and eggs. She called to me to come now to breakfast. I said to her sadly:

"Lois, I'm awfully indebted to you."

"Not on your life," said Lois. "You don't owe me anything, and if you say anything more about it, I'll get real cross. You can't imagine how nasty I am when I'm cross," she laughed. "I've had the time of my life nursing you, and Dr. Squires says—"

A beautiful flush came over Lois' face, and I said:

"Oh, Lois, I do hope you'll get married and be ever and ever so happy."

"I've got to go to England," said she. "My parents are there now, and there's a law-suit over some property a relative who died lately left. You see, I'm the real heir, they say. I'm really a ward in Chancery."

"Why, Lois, I thought you were an American."

"So I am. I was born in Massachusetts, but my mother is English, and now I've got to go over there to see about this property they say I'm rightful heir to. I'll have to leave the end of the month."

"Oh, how I'll miss you!" I cried. "I don't know how in the world I'll ever get on without you."

"When you get your strength back," said Lois, "you'll not feel that way, and you're going to stay right here and room with me till I go. So don't worry, whatever you do. Get to work now, and forget everything blue."

I had not told Lois I was a model. I had simply said that at home I had been an artist.

She had brought down my paints and palette, and now, as I arranged my things, she watched me with great interest. She had brought me a print of a basket of fruit and a bowl of flowers, and asked me if I wouldn't copy this for her. I painted them on two wooden plates she had, and she was delighted and cried out admiringly:

"Aren't you the smartest girl, though."

Tim O'Leary came in while I was painting, and the admiration of that big bartender was pathetic. He actually walked on tiptoe to come nearer to have a look. Then he said:

"I'll be back in a second."

He left the room, and returned shortly with a parcel wrapped up in white tissue paper, which he gently unfolded. He showed us a little piece of white satin with some pink flowers painted in the center, and trimmed around with cream lace; also two pieces of embroidery of a really fine quality. He handled these works of art, as he called them, poor fellow, with an almost reverent tenderness, and Lois and I loudly expressed our admiration of them.

"I'm keeping them," said Tim, "for the little girl back home. She'll be coming to me before long, and I'll have her little nest as elegant as the finest of them," he said shyly. "My Katy has eyes like this little girl here, and it's real smart you are to do such grand work, Miss Marion."

"Say, Mr. O'Leary," I said, "I'm going to make you something to add to your collection for your little girl."

I kept my word, and in a few days I had painted on a piece of blue satin that Lois found among her things a bunch of roses which poor Tim declared he could almost smell. That same evening he brought me two enormous whiskey bottles. They were about five feet high—sample bottles. They were, of course, empty. Tim made the astonishing request of me that I should paint on them, and he offered to pay me.

So I painted a little seascape on one and a wreath of lilies of the valley and forget-me-nots on the other. Of course, I would not take pay from Tim for them. The following day Tim came rushing in to tell me he had placed them on his bar, and all of his friends and customers had thought them great, and one man had offered him five dollars apiece for them. He said that nothing would induce him to part from them, but he was sending over to me all the big sample whiskey bottles he could get, and also beer and wine and champagne bottles, and he said if I would paint on these he would sell them for me. Well, the astonishing part is that he did sell them. I must have decorated at least twenty of those awful bottles, and Tim got me about forty dollars for my work. So I was able to pay Miss Darling, and I went over to the boarding-house where I still owed that bill and I paid it. To my surprise the landlady tried to force two dollars back upon me:

"We all know how sick you've been," she said, "and I said to my man: 'We'll never see the color of that board money,' and he ses: 'You'll get it yet,' and you see he's always right. So here, you can take two of it back, and may you have the good luck your pretty face should bring you."

Lois sailed on one of the small merchant liners, and it left the pier at five in the morning, so we had to get up very early to see her off. We had sat up very late the night before, and Dr. Squires had spent the evening with us and promised to be at the pier to see her off. The morning was foggy and chilly. I clung tightly to Lois before I let her go, and the doctor said:

"Here, give another fellow a chance."

He, too, kissed Lois, and there were tears in both their eyes.

XXXIX

It is inconceivably hard for a girl without a definite trade or profession, and possessed of no particular talent, to earn her own living. With Tim O'Leary's help I had made a little money that tided me over for a time, but I realized that it was merely a temporary relief. The artists would not be returning for a couple of months, and I was in a quandary what I should do. A letter from Lil Markey, the girl who had posed for Count von Hatzfeldt in Montreal, made me consider the advisability of joining her in New York.

This is Lil's letter:

Dear Marion

Here I am in little old New York. Been here two months now. I'm trying to get a job on the stage, and I've almost landed one. You ought to come on here. There's lots better opportunities, especially for a model. I have all the work I can do just now posing for the Standard, a theatrical paper.

Now, there's a fellow here who is going to get a bunch of girls and put us in living pictures. All one needs is the looks. Say, why don't you come on and join me here? I've a little flat with a couple of other girls, and we need another to squeeze in and help pay the expenses. I'd prefer you to anyone I've seen here. Say, some of them are tough though!

I was awfully sorry to hear about the old Count dying. Ada told me how cut up you were about it, too. I've a date now—my meal-ticket!

With love,
Lil

Lil's letter had started my thoughts on an old trail. The desire to act came creeping back on me. It was like an old thirst that suddenly awoke and tugged at one's consciousness to be satisfied. In Boston I had not thought to see theatrical managers. Reggie had long ago successfully squelched my ambitions in that line. Now Lil's letter and her reference to Mr. Davis quickened a new hope within me.

Perhaps, as Lil wrote, conditions were better in New York. Certainly there should be more work for a model, and perhaps I might in time really get on the stage. I had enough money for my fare and a little over, and New York appealed to me. Still, I had not definitely decided to go until after I had read the letter that came from Reggie:

DEAREST OLD GIRL (he wrote)

"I am so glad you are keeping well, and have quite recovered from your recent indisposition. I have been up to my eyes and ears in important work. I'm going to run for the next elections for the ninth ward. What do you think of that for a young and rising Barrister? I'll bet you are proud of your Reggie, now aren't you, darling? As for me, now that the rush has let up a bit, I am simply famishing for the sight of my little Marion. And *now* for the *best* news of all. I'm leaving for Boston to-morrow evening, and I'll be with you within a day! There won't be any more cross, stiff little letters coming to me from Boston, from a strange Marion that's not a bit like the loving little girl I know. The States is no place for a girl like you, darling, and I'm going there to fetch you home. Be at North station at 8.15.

Your
REGGIE

As I read Reggie's letter, strange thoughts swept turbulently over me. What was he coming for? Why should he take me back? Had the time come at last when he felt able to marry me? He had put off our marriage so long upon one excuse or another that I could not help feeling sceptical over the possibility that now the time had actually come; for his mention of his coming political fight made me wonder whether he would not be the first to think that this was a bad time for him to marry. He would need the support of the Marbridge family more than ever, and I knew that much of that support had come because of *Miss* Marbridge's personal interest in Reggie. Ada had written me that it was generally rumored in Montreal that they were engaged.

No! I felt sure Reggie was coming simply to gratify his selfish desire to see me. In his way, I knew he loved me, so far as it was possible for a man like Reggie to love, and it seemed to me that never again could I supinely be the victim of his vanity and pride. He should not come to me and pour out his confidences and his boastings; nor lavish on me caresses that could not be sincere. His influence over me had waned; and yet as I thought of his coming now, I felt a vague sense of helplessness and even terror. Might not the old influence prevail after all?

I walked up and down my miserable little room, wringing my hands and desperately trying to decide what I should do. I thought of his coming with a feeling of both longing to see him and of revulsion. I reread his letter and it seemed to me, in spite of his tender phrases, that the man's self-centered character stood out clearly in every line. All of Reggie's letters to me had laid stress upon the success of his progress both in politics and the law, and although he assumed that I would be pleased and proud, I had in reality felt fiercely resentful. I could not help comparing his circumstances and mine. I had literally been starving in Boston. I had done that thing which in the eyes at least of my own kind of people, if known to them, would have put me "beyond the pale." I had stood in a room, naked, before half a score of men! My face burned at the thought, and I suffered again the anguish I had felt when I ascended, like a slave, that model's throne.

Feverishly I packed my clothes. I would go to New York! Reggie should not again find me here to hurt me further.

My train would not leave till night and I had a few friends to whom I wished to bid good-bye. When I was leaving the house I met Tim O'Leary, and he invited me to have lunch with him. I smiled to myself as I sat opposite that bartender thinking what Reggie would say if he could see me and I suddenly said to Tim:

"Tim, do you know, you are more of a real gentleman than the grandson of a Duke I know."

Tim's broad, red face shone.

When I said good-bye to Rose St. Denis she took me in her arms like a mother.

"Enfant," she said, "you are so t'in from ze seekness, I have for you ze pity in my 'eart. I will not see your face never again, but I will make me a prayer to le bon Dieu to pitifully tek care of 'ma petite sœur.'"

"Oh, Rose," I said, crying, "I'll never, never forget *you*. I think the thought of *you* will always keep me *good*!"

I was fortunate in finding Dr. Squires in, though it was not his office hour. He seemed glad to see me and when I said:

"Doctor, I am off for New York," he answered:

"What's the matter with Boston, then?"

I explained that I thought that I could do better in New York and he agreed that my chances there were more promising. Then I said:

"Doctor, I want to thank you for all your kindness to me, and will you please tell me how much your bill is?"

He had not only come to see me two or three times a day during my illness, but he had also supplied all the medicines. He looked at me very seriously when I asked for his bill, and then he said in a deep thrilling voice:

"You do not owe me a cent. It is *I* who am indebted to *you*."

I knew what he meant, and, oh, it did thrill me to think that my illness had brought those two beautiful people together, Lois and her doctor.

When I was going out, I said:

"Doctor, I am going on the stage. Perhaps I'll succeed. Wish me good-luck."

"I wish you the best of luck in the world," he said cordially, "and I wouldn't be a bit surprised to hear of your success. You look like Dusé, Bernhardt, Julia Marlowe, and at times like a composite of all the great actresses." He did not laugh when he said that, and he wrung my hand warmly as if he actually meant it.

Once when I was a little girl, my father had punished me for something bad that I had done, and I determined to run away from home and be a gypsy. I followed an organ-grinder down the street and told him that I wanted to go with him. But he turned around and drove me back, shouting angry words at me. I crept home and hid in the barn till Charles found me there and dragged me into the house by the ear.

In running away from Reggie I had somewhat the same feeling. My heart was bursting with my love for him and at the same time with my vindictive purpose to punish him. I felt my knees trembling under me as I climbed aboard the train. Nevertheless, Reggie's influence over me seemed to vanish the farther away we got from Boston as it had when I left Montreal.

As we came into New York, I peered out of the window. The city appeared uninviting and the buildings ugly as the train passed along; nevertheless I felt already its encroaching fascination. I experienced the feelings of a child who holds a package of unknown contents in his hand, wondering and fearing to open it lest he be disappointed.

Lil lived on One hundred and ninth Street and she had sent me directions how to get there. When I came out on Forty-second Street with my valise in my hand, I did not know which way to go—which was east, west, south or north.

A man on the train, who had given me a magazine and opened the window for me, offered to carry my valise. He asked me where I was going and I told him that I wanted to find the Sixth Avenue elevated. Carrying my bag, he took me to the elevated station at Sixth Avenue and Forty-second Street. I thanked him and he said:

"It's nothing. If I had a sister arriving in a strange town alone, I'd hope some one would do as much for her."

XL

Lil had a tiny little flat near Columbus Avenue. She was delighted to see me and introduced me to the two other girls. They were both quite pretty with bright golden hair and wonderful complexions. Lil whispered to me that their hair was bleached and she said that they got their complexions from the corner drug store. I suppose in the daytime I could have seen that for myself, but I had arrived at night and I was dead tired. The girls were all very friendly and later in the evening a number of men friends called. I was too tired and sleepy to sit up with them and I went to bed. The flat was so small that I could hear them talking and they seemed to sit up all night. In spite of the noise of their chatter and laughter I went to sleep.

I stayed with Lil in that flat for a month and we all shared expenses. I got work right away with some advertising photographers who paid me five dollars for a sitting—but that would take a good part of the day. Lil and the other girls posed for the "Standard," a kind of theatrical magazine, that ran pictures of chorus girls, etc. I remember one picture which showed the girls tumbling out of a toboggan, and another where they all were supposed to have fallen out of a street-car. I could have done this work, too, but it seemed tawdry and dirty work to me and so long as I could get the photographic work I much preferred it.

In September we were all engaged to be living pictures by a man who was putting them on in vaudeville houses. The subjects represented were strictly proper ones, such as "Youth," "Psyche," "The Angelus," "Rock of Ages," etc. We received fifteen dollars a week. As we lived cheaply and men were always taking us out to dinner, our expenses were really small, and although Lil urged me to get some new clothes, I paid off my debt to Lu Frazer.

I suppose I ought to have been contented, but the work seemed stupid to me. I tired of the everlasting talk of chorus girls. They all seemed to have but one interest, and that was the stage. Mind you not *acting*, but the *stage* and all the cheap shop talk that goes with it. What is more, I was weary of Lil and her girl friends and their men friends. They sat up at the little flat so late that it was almost impossible to sleep; and there was too much drink and crazy laughter. It worked upon my nerves and I began to long for the atmosphere of the studios once more. I thought that posing for the artists was, after all, preferable to this cheap "acting." So when an offer came to me of twenty-five dollars a week as a show girl in a popular "musical show," I refused it, although Lil and the other girls exclaimed enviously over my "luck." They seemed to think that I was out of my senses and shrieked at me:

"What on earth *do* you want then?" And I replied wearily:

"I don't know myself. I guess I just want to be let alone."

How those girls did exclaim at that! Apparently, to them, I thought myself better than they were; but indeed this was not the case. I just realized that our interests were different. What seemed exciting and fine to them, seemed to me just stupid, and the miserable lot of little Willie boys who were always hovering about us with their everlasting cigarettes and silly short coats and foolish hats disgusted me. The artists for whom I had worked in Boston were *men*.

Thus I decided to leave Lil. Anyway there was some talk of their all going out with a road show and they expected to give up the flat soon.

XLI

I had had a furious letter from Reggie the day after I arrived in New York, and we had been quarreling by letter ever since. He accused me of deliberately leaving Boston when I knew that he was coming and he said: "It was a low-down trick and I shall never forgive you." In his anger he also wrote that perhaps the reason for my leaving was that I knew that he would find out the kind of life I had been living there. He wrote:

"I met a few of your 'friends'—a low-down bartender and a store clerk (Poor Billy Boyd's room-mate, I suppose) and let me compliment you on your choice of associates. Your tastes certainly have not changed."

I did not answer that first letter; but he wrote me another, apologizing, and at the same time insinuating things. To that second letter I did reply, hotly. And so it went on between us.

After leaving Lil's, I found a little room on Fifteenth Street near Eighth Avenue. It was cheap and fairly comfortable and I soon got settled there. Then I started out to look up some artists whose addresses had been sent to me by the Boston men. Right away I secured several engagements. I found, moreover, that my room was only a couple of blocks from what the artists called "Paresis Row" on Fourteenth Street. Here many artists occupied the upper floors, which had been turned into studios in these buildings, once the pretentious homes of the mighty rich people. On the lower floors various businesses were carried on.

I was sent to a man who had a studio in Paresis Row. He was a friend of Mr. Sands and although he did not use models he said he would try and help me get work. He explained to me his own kind of painting as "old-master potboilers." Sometimes, he said, he got a rush of orders for "old-masters" and then a number of fellows would get busy working on them. He declared humorously that he ran an "old-master" factory.

As I looked at his work, I felt sure I could do that kind of painting, and I said:

"Mr. Menna, would you let me try it, too?" And I told him about the work I had done for the Count and about my father, and he exclaimed:

"Fine! You're just the girl I'm looking for."

So I went to work for Mr. Menna, part of the day. I would paint in most of the start, and he would finish the pictures up; "clean them up

ONOTO WATANNA

and draw them together," as he would say. We were able this way to turn out many "old-masters." We worked for the dealers and frame-makers, who, in order to sell a frame, put these hastily made oil paintings in and sent them out as "genuine imported paintings."

Mr. Menna and I became fast friends. He treated me just like another "fellow" and divided the profits with a generous hand. Besides helping him to paint, I acted as his agent. I would go down town and see the dealers, take orders, and sometimes sell to them the ones we made on speculation.

I found out many things in the "picture business" that I had never dreamed possible, but that is another story.

At times, too, I posed for Mr. Menna. He would take spells when he became disgusted with his "potboilers," and would say he intended to do some "real stuff." These spells never lasted long, for he would run short of money, and would start with renewed energy on the "painting business" as he disgustedly called it. He discovered that I was very good at copying, but he discouraged my doing it. He said:

"There's mighty little money in copying, unless you pass it off as the original, and although the dealers do it, and I paint for them, I'm dashed if I'll actually sell them myself as original. It's not honest."

"But, Mr. Menna," I argued, "isn't it also dishonest for us to do the copying and let the dealers pass it off and sell it as original?"

"Maybe it is," he admitted, "but we don't see them selling them to the 'suckers' who buy them, and damn it all, we certainly don't get the price, so what the hell—"

Mr. Menna had raised his voice, and immediately we heard:

> *"What the hell—what the hell—what the hell!*
> *Do we care—do we care—do we care!"*

The noise came from the studio across the hall.

"It's that bunch of fellows at Fisher's," said Menna, grinning. "They get together and all chip in to pay for a model. Say, how would you like to pose for them? Most of them are illustrators, and they'd want you in street clothes and things like that. You can make an extra dollar or two. Go up and see Bonnat. He generally engages the model for the other fellows. You've met Fisher here. He's that little red-haired chap. Talk to him about it, too. Now I'm off for lunch and a glass of beer. Come along if you like, Ascough."

I went along with Menna. We ate in a little restaurant at the back of a saloon, corner of Eighth Avenue and Fourteenth Street. The lunch costs twenty-five cents each. Menna did not eat much, but he drank four glasses of beer, and he got cross with me when I at first refused to drink. So to please him I had a glass. He said:

"Now, you're a good sport, and the beer will make you fat."

"It's not my ambition to be fat," I laughed back.

"Get out," he answered. "Did you hear that German fellow who was in the studio the other day, when Miss Fleming (Miss Fleming was Mr. Menna's girl) asked him how he liked the American ladies? He said with a sad shake of his head: 'They are too t'in. The German wimmens have the proportions,' and he curved his hands in front of his chest as he said: 'It is one treat to look at her.'"

Menna laughed heartily.

"You're a German yourself," I said.

"Not on your life. I'm not," denied Menna vigorously. "I'm an American. Even my folks were born here. I studied in München. That's the place!" He shook his head and sighed.

We got up to go, and Menna told me to hustle down town and see a dealer.

XLII

Jacobs, the dealer, was busy showing some customers the paintings. The place was softly lighted, and the paintings were shown off to the best advantage by the arrangement of the lights. There were a number of Oriental rugs about, helping to make the place look luxurious, and adding somehow to the value of the paintings. Jacobs nodded to me, and I sat down to wait.

As soon as the customers were gone, he called me over and pointing to a couple of paintings in elaborate gold frames, he said:

"Those people who were in are furnishing their new home on Riverside Drive, and I expect to sell them quite a few paintings. They got stuck on those two, and I made them a price on them. Now those two are already sold, and the party who bought them wants them delivered next week. You have just come in time, Miss Ascough, as I must have these copied right away. Can you get me an artist to do it?"

I looked at the paintings. They were about sixteen by twenty-eight inches, and the subject of one à la Breton fields of wheat and harvesters, and the other was of a priest or cardinal in his red robes, sitting reading in a richly furnished library. Menna, I knew, could not possibly do the work this week, for he was working on an order for another dealer, and I had come to Jacobs to collect for old work. I thought, however, that I could easily do it myself. So I said to Jacobs:

"I know a woman artist who'll do it for you."

"A woman! No, sir! I would not have a woman do any work for me," said the dealer. "I have had all I want to do with women artists. They do much inferior work to the men, take twice as long, and get swelled heads about it. They whine if they don't make a fortune out of their daubs. No—nothing doing with the women. Now I like Menna's work. Take them to him. Don't let any one see them, and I'll very likely be able to have them copied again, as I think they'll prove good sellers."

"All right," I said, but I made up my mind to do them myself, and I went out with those precious "imported" paintings under my arm.

Mr. Menna was showing some of his "potboilers" to a man when I returned. They were paintings of little ragged boys. The man did not care for them. As he was going out he said:

"I'll come again some day when you have other pictures. Those little boy pictures are nice, and I like them, but they are not *parlor* pictures, and my customers want parlor pictures."

Menna was puffing angrily on a big cigar. I laughed as the man went out, but Menna could not see the humor of it. He got angrier and angrier. He threw down his palette and brush and let out a big original curse. Wish I could print it here.

"I hope you feel better now, Mr. Menna," I ventured.

"That's the kind of thing one is up against," he roared, "and that fool, Bonnat, was in here a while ago and told me he had refused to make some alteration in the portrait he is painting of the wife of that rich Dr. Craig, because the ass said he would not prostitute his art, and a lot of stuff like that. It makes me sick. He also lost a good chance he had to make illustrations for a magazine—best-paying magazine in New York. He had his own damned ideas about the illustrations, and as they were paying for the job they told him how they wanted them smoothed out. Bonnat belongs to the new school of painting, and he actually refused to please them—missed a chance almost any artist would be glad to get. He's a chump."

I was getting excited. In a dim way I was beginning to see something else in art than "the picture business." It reminded me of how poor Wallace, Ellen's husband, used to talk of literature. I secretly admired this Bonnat for his stand and his courage.

"Is Mr. Bonnat a Frenchman?" I asked.

"No-o." Menna seemed uncertain of his nationality, but he said after a moment: "He went to college in America. Got his Ph.D. at Harvard, and was offered a professorship out West somewhere, but after studying all those years and wasting time, he turns around and takes up art. Says all he learned about those 'ologies will enable him to paint better. Did you ever hear such rot?"

"I think I know what he means," I said eagerly.

"Oh, you do, Miss Wise-one? Well, what does he, then?" Menna was laughing at me, but I didn't mind. I felt as if I really did understand Bonnat's point of view, and I said:

"I think he means that he will understand human life better. I've heard artists in Boston discussing something about that, and I cannot explain it to myself. I only *feel* that he is right."

"Oh, rats!" answered Menna. "It's all very well if one can afford to do it. I can't, and Bonnat can't. He went without food for a whole week, except some bread and milk, and he's a big, hearty animal, and he went without his winter overcoat all last winter, because he gave it to that little consumptive Jew, Shubert. The joke of it was that Bonnat weighs nearly two hundred pounds, and little Shubert about seventy or ninety, if he weighs that, and he reaches only to Bonnat's shoulder. It was a howling joke to see him going about in that big overcoat of Bonnat's."

Suddenly there flashed over me a memory of Reggie's handsome fur-lined coat, with its rich collar of mink, and I remembered how mine had not been thick enough to keep the cruel cold out, and Reggie never even noticed how I shivered with the cold in those days. My heart went out to that big Bonnat who had given his coat to cover up a poor neighbor from the cold.

"The name is French," I said to Menna. "Are you sure he's not French?"

"His folks were originally, I believe, French Huguenots, and he's partly German. You're interested in him, aren't you? Better not waste your time on a nut," and Menna finally dismissed Bonnat with a laugh.

When I showed him the paintings he said that I could copy them as well as he could, and made me sit right down and go to work.

Somehow, as I copied those paintings, the pleasure was spoiled for me. There kept running into my head thoughts about *honesty in painting*, and again I recalled my brother-in-law's remarks on literature, and I knew that it must be the same with all art. I could not get my mind off that man who would not for money be untrue to himself. I felt something stirring within me that I had never stopped to think of before. And I began to despise myself for the work I was doing, and I think I would have despised Menna, too; but suddenly I thought of my father, and I wanted to cry. I realized that there were times when we literally had to do the very things we hated. Ideals were luxuries that few of us could afford to have. Menna had said we had to live, and that was true enough. Most of us were destined to wade through, not above, the miry quicksands of life. Art then was only for the few and the rare and the fortunate.

Menna himself had had great promise as a youth. Moreover, his parents were wealthy, and they had sent him to study in Munich. But when his father died, there was found scarcely enough money left to support his mother and sisters, and Menna was sent for to do his share.

He was only twenty-eight, and he tried to support himself with his brush. He was a good-natured, careless fellow, whose path had hitherto been smoothed for him, and so he chose the easiest way in art. He drifted into the potboiler painting, and alas! there he stayed, as is generally the case.

XLIII

I finished my copies in four days, and they were scarcely dry when I carried them down to Jacobs. He examined them as if he were buying some material by the yard. I felt very nervous as he looked at them. Then he grunted, went over to his desk and wrote me a check for thirty dollars and fifteen cents. Menna told me he sold them for a couple of hundred if not more. He handed me the check with the remark:

"They will do. It takes a *man* to do a piece of work right."

For a time Menna had very little work for me. There were slack times when he had not enough for himself, and he would get very discouraged. Sometimes he would gather up all the paintings he had made and say:

"Go and slaughter them to those damned frame-makers, Ascough, and sell them for what you can get—anything."

I would remonstrate with him, and point out that if he would wait and not be in such a hurry for his money we could get better prices.

"Hang it all," he would shout, "what's the use?"

So long as he had a few dollars to sit at some table with friends and order beer, he would sacrifice, or as he called it "slaughter," anything and everything.

As work was now very scarce, I decided to see Fisher about the posing. So I went across the hall and knocked at his door.

"Hello, Miss Ascough," he called out cheerily, as I came in. "Come on in and sit down. You seem pretty busy in Menna's studio. What are you doing for him?"

"Oh, I help him paint," I said, "and sell his work for him, and sometimes I pose. That's what I want to ask you about now. Wouldn't you like me to pose for you and your friends? I hear you all sketch together once a week."

"We'll be glad to have you," he declared cordially, his eye scanning me admiringly. "Why didn't you speak before?"

"Well, I've been pretty busy with Mr. Menna, but work's slack now. So, if you like, I can give you some time."

"Good. See Bonnat about it. He generally engages the model, and we're to work in his room next time. Have you met him?"

"No."

"Well, I guess you have *heard* him," laughed Fisher. "He certainly makes enough noise. When he first moved in here, we used to be wakened up early in the morning by him stamping up the stairs from the bathroom, carrying his bucket of water. There's no water on his floor, and the way he stamped and cussed as he went up those two flights of stairs was enough to awaken the dead, and all the stairs would be splashed with water. We thought that cross old Mary, the caretaker, would go for him (as she *can*), but she never said a word to him. Just went to work and wiped up the water every morning. That comes of being a good-looker."

"Is he so handsome, then?"

Fisher himself was a homely, red-haired little fellow.

"You bet he is," he said, "as handsome as they make 'em, so don't get stuck on him, as we want to keep Bonnat here. What's more, he paints like he looks—great! wonderful! He'll make his mark yet. Go along and see him now. 'Raus mit you!'"

So, leaving Fisher's studio, I climbed the stairs to the top floor, and, turning to the left, I saw a door with a card nailed on it, bearing the name of Paul Bonnat. I stood and looked at the door for some time, and then I knocked. The door was opened with a jerk, and standing in the doorway was a young giant, whose head seemed to reach the top of the door. His hair was all sticking up. It was fair, and the eyes that looked at me questioningly were blue. He had a wide, clever mouth, and a chin that was like a cleft rock. As I stared up at him, his face smiled all over, so that I was forced to smile in return, and I thought to myself:

"Why, he looks like a young viking." Somehow he made me think of my father, in coloring and the northern type of face, but this man had a more distinct personality that seemed almost to strike one. Papa was gentle and a dreamer. Bonnat was vitally alive.

"Mr. Fisher told me you wanted a model."

He nodded and his big glance, still smiling, looked me over.

"Come in, come in."

He was about twenty-six or seven, and in spite of the two hundred pounds Menna told me he weighed, he was not the least bit fat.

I was now in the room, and I glanced about me. Never have I seen such an untidy room in my life. It was not dirty, but simply littered up with things.

"Sit down," he said, sweeping off some drawings and papers on to the floor from a chair that was loaded. There was also a glass of water on the chair, and he tipped that off, too, and the water ran on the floor.

"Oh," I gasped, "do you always throw everything on the floor like that?"

"Not everything," he answered, grinning. Then he handed me a box of cigarettes. I took one, and he began to look for a match. On the couch, the table and on all the chairs were piled papers, paints, brushes, clothes, boots and all manner of articles. It looked as if he never put anything where it belonged. Even his clothes were not hung up. On the walls were sketches, paintings, a pair of fencing swords, and the floor could scarcely be seen, as it also was covered with articles, and there were boxes of cigarette stumps and several empty glasses and bottles. As he hunted for the matches, he tumbled one thing after another on the floor.

I was possessed with a desire to tidy up that room. My hands were literally itching to go to work upon it. He seemed so helpless among all his belongings.

"Got it at last!" he laughed, as he discovered the box of matches on the window sill, and, striking one, he offered me a light. I never cared for smoking, but as I was always expected to smoke I usually accepted to save the bother of refusing and being urged.

"It's the devil to be in such a small hole," he said. "I seem to spend all my time looking for things. Well, now, let's see. You're going to pose for us, are you? Is next Sunday all right, or do you have to go to confess something?" He asked the question teasingly, as if he enjoyed poking fun at me.

"No, I never go to church," I admitted.

A shocked look came into his face, and he opened his mouth wide.

"What? You are a heathen!"

He threw back his head and burst into the loudest and most infectious laughter I have ever heard.

"Then it's all settled," he said. "Now I have to go to lunch. Want to come along and have a bum lunch with me?"

I nodded, and he said: "Good!" hunted around for his hat, stuck it jauntily on his head, and, taking me by the arm, we went down the stairs.

When we were sitting in the little restaurant near Sixth Avenue, he asked me a lot of questions about myself, and before I knew it I had told him all about my father and mother and brothers and sisters and the work I had done in Montreal. Then I told him of the hard times I had in Boston. He seemed intensely interested, and when I got through he rattled off a lot of hard-luck stories about the artists, and told me something about the exigencies and makeshifts that all of them had had. He'd tell one story of hard luck after another, not as if it were something to feel badly about, but as if it were the common lot of every one. I think he did that so I wouldn't think I myself had been especially singled out by fate.

He told me how only a few months before Fisher and he and "a couple of other guys" were all "broke," and none of them had enough cash to buy a separate meal-ticket which entitled him to six meals for one dollar and a quarter, instead of twenty-five cents each meal. So they had all chipped in together and bought one ticket between them on the third of July. Well, when they went to dinner on the fourth of July to the Little Waldorf on Eighth Avenue, they were confronted by this sign:

"The landlord has gone away for a holiday, and will return next week."

Bonnat seemed to think that an immense joke. He said every one in Paresis Row had had some such experience.

He wanted to know where I lived and I told him Fifteenth Street, and then he asked suddenly:

"Alone?" When I answered "yes" he smiled beamingly at me. Then he took me home, and lifting his hat in going, said:

"You're engaged then. Sunday. Good-bye." I could see him striding down the street, his head up, and his broad shoulders thrown back. He whistled as he went along.

XLIV

Sunday morning was bleak and cold. It had been raining for the last three days, and as I crossed the corner of Eighth Avenue and Fourteenth Street the puddles were so deep that I splashed the mud all over my raincoat. It was cold and chilly when I reached Paul Bonnat's studio.

There were, besides Fisher and Paul Bonnat, two other men, one named Enfield, who was an illustrator, and a Mr. Christain, who worked as a lithographer on week days and painted in his spare time on Sundays.

When I got in Fisher seized me by the arm, and with a mock of proud gesture he showed me Bonnat's renovated room:

"Look, Miss Ascough. Can you beat this for a studio de luxe—and all in your honor! Gee! Look at that beautiful pile of rubbish he has swept under the table there, where he thought you wouldn't see it. He's trying to impress you with the beauty of his home."

"Shut up!" shouted Bonnat. "I'm the only one of the bunch who patronizes the bath here at any rate."

"Ugh!" shuddered Fisher. "That bath is filthy, and there's never a drop of hot water, so one would be dirtier after taking a bath there."

"Nonsense!" answered Bonnat. "All you have to do is to take down a pitcher or a bucket. Then rub soap all over your body, and stand up in the tub and pour the pitchers of cold water over and over yourself. It's fine!"

"Whoor-roo!" shivered Enfield. "No cold water for me!"

Enfield was a thin-faced, sensitive-looking fellow, with eyes that lighted up unexpectedly, and who seemed to shrink up in his clothes, as if he were always cold. Menna had told me he was very talented, and could make big money at illustrations, but he drank all the time, not in a noisy way, but in a sad, quiet, secret way. He lived in a room somewhere on the East side in the tenement-house district. It was almost empty, except for an old stove, and Enfield would collect all the newspapers he could lay his hands on, and he slept on a pile of these, with another pile on top of him, and in bitter cold weather when he could not afford other fuel he burned his papers. He would roll them into tight logs and they would smoulder just like wood for hours, and give out a good heat even. His room was simply piled with old newspapers, said Menna.

This man had come from extremely refined and wealthy people, but he chose to live in this dreadful way, so as to indulge his vice for liquor, and, it was suspected, drugs. At times he would brace up and do a decent piece of work, and then he would turn up, dressed immaculately, and the boys would be treated to the best of everything; but inside of a week he would spend every cent and pawn his clothes. I liked Enfield, though sometimes his cadaverous face frightened me. His hands always looked so thin and cold that I had a kind of maternal desire to take them in mine and warm them. There was something pathetically helpless about all these artists. They seemed all boys to me—even the older ones. I suppose it was that childish helplessness about them that appealed most to me.

They all chatted away, and gibed each other and joked as they worked, and they would tell stories, and then all stop work to laugh uproariously. Fisher told one about Enfield. He said that one evening the boys had a little spread in their rooms, beer and sausage and cheese, and for a joke they had put the remains of the sausage and cheese in the pocket of Enfield's coat. Enfield caught up the story here and finished it thus:

"Some time later, I was starving." He said that as if it were quite the usual thing to starve a bit. "I hadn't eaten for two days, and all of a sudden I put my hand in that pocket, and found a sausage and some cheese. It surely saved my life."

All of their stories were a curious mixture of tragedy and exquisite humor, and while I laughed one minute my eyes would fill up the next. I suppose, after all, that's just how life is really compounded—of tragedy and comedy. It's good to be able to feel both of these elements in our lives. A writer once referred to some of his characters as: "*dead* people"— dead in the sense of simply being unable to grasp at any significance in life save the dull living from day to day. It seems to me one does not regret passing through scorching fires. It's the only way one can get the big vision of life. I used to feel bitter, when I contemplated the easy life of other girls, and compared it with my own hard battle. Now I know that, had I to go through it all again, I would not exchange my hard experiences for the luxury that is the lot of others. I can even understand what it is to pity and not envy the rich. They *miss so much.* Money cannot buy that knowledge of humanity that comes only to him who has lived among the real people in the world—the poor!

All of which is what Bonnat would call "beside the question"— digression, that has "nothing to do with the thing, tra la!"

"Do you see that piece of drapery, Miss Ascough?" said Mr. Christain. "Well, Bonnat bought that yesterday at a little Jew shop on Third Avenue where they have several prices for everything. He asked: 'What's the price,' and the Jew gave him the top-notch: 'ninety-eight cent one yard,' said he. 'Ninety-eight cents!' shouted that big chump there, 'that's dirt cheap! I'll take it!' He could have got it for fifteen, and when the Jew was wrapping it up, I could see by his face that he was sorry he hadn't charged ninety-nine. Can you beat him for an easy mark?"

"Strikes me," growled Bonnat, "we're not particularly easy on Miss Ascough. She's been posing over her time."

"True enough," said Fisher.

"Well, what's the verdict?" demanded Bonnat, beaming down upon me. "Shall we have her next week, or get a nice little soft blonde in?"

I thought he was talking seriously, and I said:

"Oh, I hope you'll have me. I like posing for you all."

"You do?" said Bonnat, and then he added roughly: "It's damned hard work, isn't it?"

I said:

"Not with fellows like you. I forgot I was posing. I like to hear you all talk."

They all laughed at that, and seemed much pleased. So then I was engaged to come again the following Sunday, to "hear them all talk."

XLV

I had been posing for several Sundays for the "Club" in Paresis Row. At first, all four of the men came regularly. Then Enfield dropped out, then Christain, who was out of work, and finally one Sunday when I arrived I found only Bonnat there. He insisted that I should remain, as, he said, he was very much in need of a model.

He had been working away, without speaking once to me for some time. It was funny to watch his face while he worked, making curious facial expressions and attitudes corresponding to certain expressions and emotions. When he was through, I went over and looked at the painting, and I thought it was very wonderful. I said shyly:

"If you like, I'll take it to some of the dealers I sell Mr. Menna's paintings to, and Mr. Bonnat"—I wanted him to know that I, too, could paint, but I had never the courage to tell him before all the other men—"I sometimes sell some of my own, too."

He turned around slowly and looked at me.

"So you paint, too, do you?"

I nodded.

After a moment, he said:

"We won't bother about those dealers you speak of, but I'd like to see your work."

"I get ten dollars for a painting sometimes," I said, thinking that would be an added inducement to him to let me help him sell his paintings. He smiled when I said that and after a moment he said:

"Ten dollars are a mighty comfortable thing, and so are two pairs of darned socks, as Oliver Twist would have said; but there's something besides the selling question in all these efforts of ours—don't you know that?"

"You mean self-expression?" I asked timidly. I had heard studio talk before.

"Yes—self-expression, and a good many other things besides."

He paused, studying me musingly.

"I wonder if you will understand," he said almost to himself, and then he added, with a beaming look: "Yes, I am sure you will. It's this way: If our art is our life, then perhaps we had best follow Goethe's advice and live resolutely in the good, the whole and the true. To do that we must know *values*—values on the canvas and values in life."

Reggie's scale of values flashed to my mind.

"To be well informed," he went on, "generally helps us to recognize values."

"The value of one's paintings?" I asked slyly.

"I have an inclination to regard you as a little mouse," he said, "but if you bite like that, I shall call you a flea instead. Yes, that value, and the value of money, too, by—hearsay."

As he talked I had a sense of excitement, a certain uplifting thrill, as it were. It seemed to me he was opening the doors into a world that I had previously merely sensed. I knew dimly of its existence. The girls at Lil's had said: "Well, what *do* you want then?" I did not know myself. I think it was simply a blind, intuitive reaching after the light of understanding. I *felt* these things, but I could not express my needs. I was of the inarticulate, but not the unfeeling. Bonnat must have realized this quality in me, else he would not have revealed himself so freely to me. He talked with an odd mixture of seriousness and lightness. It was almost as if he slowly chose his words, to make himself clear, just as if he were speaking to a child—a child he was not entirely sure of, but whom he wanted to reach.

"I do know what you mean," I cried. "Do you know Kipling's 'L'Envoi?'—because that expresses it exactly."

"Let's hear it."

And I recited warmly, for I loved it:

> "When earth's last picture is painted
> And the tubes are twisted and dry,
> When the oldest colors are faded,
> And the youngest critic has died,
> We shall rest, and, faith, we shall need it—
> Lie down for an æon or two,
> Till the Master of all good workmen
> Shall set us to work anew.
> And those who are good shall be happy;
> They shall sit in a Golden Chair;
> They shall splash at a ten-league canvas
> With brushes of Comet's hair;
> They shall find real saints to draw from—
> Magdalene, Peter and Paul;
> They shall work for an age at a sitting,

And never be tired at all;
And only the Master shall praise us,
And only the Master shall blame;
And no one shall work for money,
And no one shall work for Fame:
But each for the joy of the working;
And each in his separate star
Shall draw the thing as he sees it
For the God of Things as They are!"

"Bully!" cried Bonnat. "Your dramatic training was not lost. Only one thing—"

"What?"

He put his two hands on my shoulders, and gave me a friendly little shake and hug:

"You—lithp!" (lisp) he said.

Before I could protest at that deadly insult he took my hands and squeezed them hard, and he said:

"I believe we speak the same language after all. We *think* it, anyway, don't we?"

XLVI

I had been posing all afternoon. Bonnat still insisted on my coming each Sunday, although the other men were through with me for the time being. I was not sure that Bonnat could really afford to have a model alone, and I often thought I should not go; but somehow I found myself unable to keep away. All week long I looked forward to that afternoon in Paul Bonnat's studio, and the thought that they could not last made me feel very badly.

"Look at the time!" He pointed dramatically to the clock on the shelf. It was upside down. Then he regarded me remorsefully:

"You must be tired out, and hungry, too. What do you say to having dinner with me to-night? How about one of those awful Italian table-d'hotes, where they give you ten courses with red ink for the price of a sandwich? Will that suit you?"

I was seized with a distaste to go out in the rain, even with Bonnat, to one those melancholy restaurants. I looked about me, and sighing, said:

"I wish I had a place to cook. I'm awfully tired of restaurants."

"What, can you cook?" he demanded excitedly, just as if he had discovered some miraculous talent in me.

"Why, yes," I said proudly. "And I love to, too. I can cook anything," I added sweepingly.

"You don't say." His eyes swept the room. "Where's that trunk?" He found it, and called to me to come and see what it contained.

"See here—how's this? I brought these things with me when I first left home, and intended to cook for myself, but a fellow can't bother with these things. Hasn't got the time, and then everything gets lost about the place," he added ruefully. "Now here's a little gas stove. I use it to heat water for shaving, and sometimes when the boys come in on a cold night we make a hot drink."

I had picked up a little brass kettle, and I saw him looking at it. He put his hands on the other side of it gently, and he said:

"That belonged to my mother. She's been dead two years now."

"Oh, we'll not touch it," I declared. "We'll make coffee in something else."

He pressed the little kettle upon me.

"No, no, you shall make it in this. My mother would have liked you to. I wish you could have known her."

"I wish I could," I said earnestly. Bonnat stared at me a moment, and then he said, moving toward the door:

"I'm going to the delicatessen, and I'll bring back what?"

"Anything that is not cooked," I said. "I do so want to cook a real dinner, and there's a couple of pans here though I wish there was more than one gas thing."

While he was gone I went quickly to work. I fairly flew about that studio, putting everything to rights, piling up the things in their proper places, hanging up the things that should be hung, and sweeping, tidying, dusting, till it really looked like a different place. Then I set the table with two plates I found in his trunk, one teaspoon, one knife and two forks. There was only one cup between us, but there were two glasses. Presently Bonnat came in with his arms full of packages. He stood in the doorway, just looking about him, and slowly over his face there came the most beautiful smile I have ever seen in the world. Somehow it just seemed to embrace the whole room, and me, too. He set the packages down, and this is what he had bought: Frankfurters, cheese, eggs, butter, bread, pickles, jam, and a lot of other things, but not a thing to cook except the frankfurters. I must have looked disappointed, for he asked anxiously:

"Isn't it all right?"

"Oh, I had set my mind on making a rice pudding," I said.

"That's all right," he declared eagerly. "You shall, too. What do you need for it?"

"Well, rice, cinnamon, sugar, milk, eggs and butter."

He laughed, and went singing and rattling down the stairs on his second errand. I could hear him when he came back all the way from the entrance of the building; but I loved his noise!

I made that pudding. As we had no oven, I had to boil it, but I put cinnamon heavily on top, so it looked as if browned, and it did taste good. We were both so tired of the cheap restaurants that everything tasted just fine, and Bonnat leaned over the table and fervently declared that I was the best cook he had ever met in his life. We were both laughing about that, when after a rat-tat on the door, it burst open and in came Fisher. He stopped short and stared at us.

"Well, upon my word, you look like newly-weds," he said, and that made me blush so that I pretended to drop something and leaned over to pick it up, for I was ashamed to look at Paul Bonnat after that.

"My, but it smells good," said Fisher. "Got a bite for another beggar, Miss Ascough?" Then his eye went slowly and amazedly about the room, and he exclaimed: "Gee whiz! Have the fairies been to work? Well, you certainly look cozy now."

He drew up a chair, and went to work on the remnants of our feast, talking constantly as he ate.

"Say, Miss Ascough, we fellows can have lots of spreads like this, now that we know you can cook."

"What do you take her for?" growled Bonnat. "Do you think the whole hungry bunch of you are going to have her cooking for you? Not on your life, you're not."

Fisher laughed.

"By the way, there's a bunch of us going down to the Bowery to-morrow night. We'll get chop suey at a pretty good joint there, and then we're going to Atlantic Garden where we can get those big steins of beer. Why don't you bring Miss Ascough along?"

Bonnat leaned over the table and asked:

"*Will* you go with me?" just as if I would be conferring a great favor on him, and I said that I would. After that I was included in all their little trips, and sometimes I would try to pretend I was a boy, too; only there was Paul, and somehow when I looked at Paul, I was glad I was a girl.

XLVII

I was helping Menna that day. He had been very busy, and I had been working for him both mornings and afternoons. He had told me, however, that soon he expected to "pick up and go West," and I was troubled about that. I depended upon Menna for most of my work, and we got along splendidly together. As I have said, Menna had always treated me just like a "fellow" as he would call it.

There was a knock at the door, and in came Paul Bonnat. After nodding to Menna, he strolled over to where I was working and stood at the back of me, watching me paint.

"She's quite a painter," he said after a moment to Menna, who looked up and nodded, and said:

"Yes, she does quite O. K."

After a while Menna turned around on his stool and asked:

"Got anything on to-night, Bonnat?"

"No—nothing particular."

"Well, a lady friend of mine is coming in from Staten Island, and I promised to take her somewhere to supper and see the town. Can't you and Miss Ascough join us?"

Bonnat beamed, just as if Menna had handed him a gift, and he said:

"Sure, if Miss Ascough will go with me."

I said that I would. I think I would have gone with him anywhere he asked me to.

"Meet us here at seven, then," said Menna, returning to his work.

"All right. Good-bye." Bonnat went out, slamming the door noisily behind him. We could hear him singing the "Preislied" from "Meistersinger" as he went up the stairs. He had a big, wonderful baritone voice. We stopped painting to listen to him, but when I turned to resume my work, I found Menna watching me. He said:

"You and Bonnat are getting pretty friendly, eh?"

I felt myself color warmly, but I tried to laugh, and said:

"Oh, no more than I am with any of the other boys."

Menna had his thumb through his palette, and he stared at me hard. Then he said suddenly:

"Gee! What a fool I was to let him get ahead of me."

He set down his palette, and came over to my stool:

"Say, Marion" (he had never called me Marion before), "you and I would make a corking good team. Suppose we pair off together to-night, and we'll put Miss Fleming on to Bonnat? What do you say?"

"Mr. Menna, you had better stick to your own girl," I said, feeling uneasy. Menna continued to stare down at me and as he said nothing to that, I added:

"You know you and I are just partners in our work, and don't let's fool. It'll spoil everything."

"Oh, all right," said he, "I don't have to get down on my knees to you or any other girl."

He had never spoken to me like that before. Until this day, he had never asked me to go anywhere with him, nor tried to see me after work hours, and I did not suppose he was the least bit interested in me, and I supposed he was quite settled with his own sweetheart. I was so glad when Miss Fleming knocked on the door.

That evening we all went to Shefftel Hall. It was one of the oldest places in New York, and was interesting because of the class of people who patronized the place and its resemblance to the German gardens, which it was in fact itself. There were German ornaments and steins all around the place on a high shelf. There was an excellent orchestra which played good selections and Bonnat hummed when they played some of his favorites. Menna and Bonnat seemed to differ on almost every subject, and Menna seemed in a savagely contrary mood that night.

Bonnat would explain his point of view about something, and Menna would say irritably:

"Yes, yes, but what's the use?"

Bonnat said that a man should show in his work the human mood, and that a picture should mean something more than a pretty melody of colors. Menna interrupted him with:

"What's the use, as long as we get good Pilsener beer?"

Paul laughed at that, and called to a waiter to bring some more Pilsener for Menna right away. After the dinner was over, Mr. Menna took Miss Fleming home, and Paul and I walked up Fourteenth Street, stopping to look in the windows, and to glance at the curious people in the throngs that passed us. Fourteenth Street was then a very gay and bedizened place at night.

When we reached my door, Paul, who had been very silent, took my hand and held it for some time, without saying a word. I could feel his eyes looking down on me in the darkness of the street, and somehow the very clasp of his hand seemed to be speaking to me, telling me things that made me feel warm, and, oh! so happy. When he did speak at last, his big voice was curiously repressed, and he said huskily:

"I think I know now why some men give up art for the sake of protecting their *own*!" He said "own" with such strange emphasis, pressing my hand as he said it, that I felt too moved to answer him, and I had a great longing to put my arms around him and draw his head down to mine.

After that night Mr. Menna did not seem the same to me. All the little kindnesses I had been accustomed to receive from him, such as cleaning my palette, my brushes, and nailing my canvases on the stretchers, he now let me do myself, and once when I asked him to varnish a painting of mine, he answered:

"Why don't you get that Bonnat to do it for you?"

XLVIII

Dear Marion

Mr. Hirsh is going to put on the living pictures in Providence for two weeks, and he says he would like to take the same girls that he had before, and told me to tell you that he will pay twenty dollars a week. Also that he will take us to Boston and some other places if we do well in Providence.

Why don't you come and see us to-night? and bring along the fellow Hatty said she saw you walking with on Fourteenth St. How are you anyway?—I'm leaving for Providence to-morrow.

With love,
Lil

I had been thinking of Lil's letter all day, but I could not make up my mind how to answer it. The thought of making forty dollars in two weeks appealed to me very much, for we were not very busy now, and Menna expected to go West very soon. On account of my work with Menna I had not done much posing in New York, but I intended to call on some artists and see about engagements when Menna should go. Forty dollars was a lot of money to me, and it would take me many weeks to earn that much in posing. It did seem as if I simply could not refuse this chance. But my mind kept turning to Paul Bonnat. I could think of nobody else but him. He had made my life worth while. I thought of all the happy times we had together. He did not have much money to spend on me, and he could not take me to expensive places like Reggie used to, but he lived as I did, and we enjoyed the same things—things that Reggie would have called silly and cheap. We went to the exhibitions of the artists, long walks in the park, to the Metropolitan Museum, and, best of all, to the opera. That was the one thing Paul would be extravagant about, although our seats were in the top gallery of the family circle. I would be out of breath by the time I climbed up there, but I learned to appreciate and love the best only in music, just as Paul was teaching me to understand the best in all art.

There, I listened with mingled feelings and enjoyment to the operas of Wagner. His "Tristan und Isolde" rang in my ears for days, and by the time I heard "Die Meistersinger," I was able thoroughly to enjoy what before had been unknown land to me. We Canadians had never gone much beyond a little of Mendelssohn, which the teachers of music seemed to consider the height of classical music, and the people were still singing the old sentimental songs, not the ragtime the Americans love, but the deadly sweet melodies that cloy and teach us nothing. Of course, no doubt, things have changed there now; but it was that way when I was a girl in Montreal.

I did not want to leave New York even for two weeks. I had begun to love my life here. There was something fine in the comradeship with the boys in the old ramshackle studio building. I had been accepted as one of the crowd, and I knew it was Bonnat's influence that made them all treat me as a sister. Fisher once said that a "fellow would think twice before he said anything to me that wasn't the straight goods," and he added, "Bonnat's so darned *big*, you know."

I had often cooked for all of the boys in the building. We would have what they called a "spread" in Bonnat's or Fisher's studio, and they would all come flocking in, and fall to greedily upon the good things I had cooked. I felt a motherly impulse toward them all, and I wanted to care for and cook for—yes—and wash them, too. Some of the artists in that building *were pretty dirty*.

Paul had never spoken of love to me, and I was afraid to analyze my feelings for him. Reggie's letters were still pouring in upon me, and they still harped upon one thing—my running away from him in Boston. He kept urging me to come home, and lately he had even hinted that he was coming again to fetch me; but he said he would not tell me when he would come, in case I should run off again.

I used to sit reading Reggie's letters with the queerest sort of feelings for, as I read, I would not see Reggie in my mind at all, but Paul Bonnat. It did seem as if all the things that Reggie said that once would have pierced and hurt me cruelly had now lost their power. I had even a tolerant sort of pity for Reggie, and wondered why he should trouble any longer to accuse me of this or that, or even to write to me at all. I am sure I should not have greatly cared if his letters had ceased to come. And now as I turned over in my mind the question of leaving New York, I thought not of Reggie, but of Paul. It is true, I might only be away for the two weeks in Providence; on the other hand, I realized that should we succeed there, I would be foolish not to go on with the troupe to Boston. I decided finally that I would go.

I went over especially to tell Paul about it. I said:

"Mr. Bonnat, I'm going away from New York, to do some more of that—that living-picture work." I waited a moment to see what he would say—he had not turned around—and then I added, as I wanted to see if he really cared—"Maybe I won't come back at all."

He stood up, and took me by the shoulders, making me look straight at him.

"How long are you to be gone?" he demanded, as if he had penetrated my ruse.

"Two weeks in Providence," I said, "but if we succeed, we go on to Boston and—"

"Promise me you'll come back in two weeks. Promise me that," he said.

He was looking straight down into my eyes, and I think I would have promised him anything he asked me to; so I said in a little weak voice:

"I promise."

"Good!" he replied. "I would not let you go, if it were in my power to stop you, but I know you need the money, and I have no right to deprive you of it. Oh, good God! it's *hell* not to be able to—" He broke off, and gently took my hands up in his:

"Look here, little mouse. There's a chance of my being able to make a big pot of money. I'll know in a few days' time. Then you shall not have to worry about anything. But as I am now fixed, why I can't stop you from anything. I haven't the right."

I wanted to tell him that he could stop me from going if he wanted to; but he had not told me he cared for me, and there was a possibility that I was mistaken about him. He had that big, gentle way with every one, and it might be that I had mistaken his kindly interest in me for something that he did not really feel. So I laughed now lightly, and I said:

"Oh, I'll be back soon, and if you like you can see me off on the train."

When we were in the Grand Central the following night, I tried to appear cheerful, but I could not prevent the tears running down my face, and when finally he took my hand to say good-bye, I said:

"Oh, it's dreadful for me to say this; b-but if I don't see you soon again I—t-think I will die."

He bent down when I said that and kissed me right on my lips, and he did not seem to care whether every one in the station saw us or not. Then I knew that he did love me, and that knowledge sent me flying blindly down the platform. After I was aboard, I found I had taken the wrong train to Providence. I should have taken an earlier or a later one. Lil was already there, and was to have met me at the station from the earlier train, but the train I had taken would not get in till four in the morning.

When I arrived in Providence I did not know where to go. I had Lil's address, but she had written me she was living at a "very respectable house" where the people would have been terribly shocked to know she was a model, and I felt I could not go there at such an hour in the morning. The rain was coming down in torrents. A colored boy was carrying my bag, and he asked me where I wanted to go. Indeed, I did not know. When I hesitated, he said that the hotels didn't take ladies alone, but that he knew of an all-night restaurant where I could get something hot to eat and I could stay there till morning. So he took me over to Minks'. I had often eaten in Minks' restaurant in Boston, and the place looked quite familiar to me. I had a cup of hot coffee and a sandwich, and then I asked the waitress if there was some place where I could go and freshen or clean up a bit. She whispered to the man at the desk, and he nodded, and then she beckoned to me to follow her. We went upstairs to a sort of loft. It was bare, save of packing cases, but she showed me to a little cracked looking-glass where she said I could do my hair. I told her I had been on the train all night, and she said sympathetically:

"Sure, you look it."

I went over to Lil's boarding-house about seven in the morning. She was right near Minks', and said I was foolish not to have come right over.

Well, we played every night in the theatre in Providence, and we made what theatrical people call a "hit." The whole town turned out to see us. The girls were all as pleased as could be, and so was Mr. Hirsch, and they made all kinds of plans for the road tour, but I could think of nothing but New York, and I was so lonely, in spite of the noisy company of the girls, that I used to go over and look at the railway tracks that I knew ran clear to New York. And I thought of Paul! I thought of Paul every single minute. The little maid would slip his letters every morning under my door, and I used to cry and laugh before I even opened them and I held them to my lips and face, and I kept them all in the bosom of my dress, right next to me.

We had finished our engagement. Lil and I were coming out of the dressing-room the last night when somebody slapped me on the back. I turned around, and there was Mr. Davis. He was so glad to see me that he nearly wrung my hand off, and he insisted on walking home with us. He told me he was now manager of a theatrical company, and that he had been looking around for me ever since Lil told him I was in New York.

"Now, Marion," he said, "you are going to begin where you left off in Montreal, and it's up to you to make good. You've got it in you, and I want to be the man to prove it."

I asked him what he meant, and he said he was starting a new "show" in Boston that week, and that he had a part for me that would give me an opportunity.

I said faintly:

"I was going back to New York to-morrow."

Lil exclaimed:

"What're you talking about? Aren't you going along with Mr. Hirsch?"

"Instead of going to New York," said Mr. Davis, "you come along with me to Boston. Cut out this living-picture stuff. It's not worthy of you. I always said there was the right stuff in you, Marion, and now I'm going to give you the chance to prove it."

For a moment an old vision came back to me. I saw myself as "Camille," the part I had so loved when little more than a child in Montreal, and I felt again the sway of old ambitions. I said to Mr. Davis:

"Oh, yes, I think I *will* go with you!"

But when I got back to my room, I took out Paul's last letter. How confident he was of my keeping my promise to return! He wrote of all the preparations he was making, and he said he had a stroke of luck, and that I should share it with him. We should have dinner at Mouquin's, and then we would see some show, or the opera. Whatever we did, or wherever we went we would be together.

I got out my little writing pad, and I wrote a letter hurriedly to Mr. Davis:

Dear Mr. Davis

"Will you please excuse me, but I have to go to New York. I'll let you know later about acting."

I sent the note to Mr. Davis by the little maid in the house, and he sent back a sheet with this laconic message upon it:

"Now or never—Give me till morning."

Lil talked and talked and talked to me all night about it, and she seemed to think I was crazy not to grab this chance that had come to me, and she said any one of the other girls would have gone clean daft about it. She said I was a little fool, and never knew when opportunity came in my way. "Just look," she said, "how you turned down that chance you had to be a show girl, and all of us other girls weren't even asked, and I'll bet our legs are as pretty as yours. It's just because you've got a sort of—of—well, I heard a man call it 'sex-appeal' about you, but you're foolish to throw away your good chances, and by and by they won't come to you. You'll be fat and ugly."

I said:

"Oh, Lil, stop it. I guess I know my business better than you do."

"Well, then, answer me this," said Lil, sitting up in bed, "are you engaged to that fellow who sends you letters every day?"

I could not answer her.

"Well, what about Reggie Bertie?"

"For heaven's sakes, go to sleep," I entreated her, and with a grunt of disgust she at last turned over.

Next morning Paul's letter fully decided me. It said that he would be at the station to meet me! He was expecting me, and I must not, on any account, fail him.

"Lil, wake up! Wake up!" I cried, shaking her by the arm. "I'm going to take the first train back to New York."

Lil answered sleepily:

"Marion, you always were crazy."

All of a sudden the room turned red on all sides of us, and I realized that it was on fire. The little stove had a pipe with an elbow in the wall, and when I put a match to the kindling, the flames must have crept up to the thin wooden walls from the elbow, and in an instant the wall had ignited. I had on only a nightdress. I seized the quilt off the bed, and threw it on the flames, but it seemed only to serve as fresh fuel. Lil was crouched back on the bed, petrified with terror, and literally unable to move. Desperately screaming, "Fire, fire!" I seized the pitcher and flung it at the flames, and then somehow I grabbed hold of Lil by the hand, and both shrieking, we ran out into the hall. Then I fainted. When I came to, the fire was out, and the landlady and her son and husband and Lil were all standing over me, laughing and crying.

"Well," said the man, "did you try to burn us out?" He turned to his wife, and said: "It's a good job I got that insurance, eh?"

My clothes were not burned, but soaking wet, and so I missed my train—the train that Paul was going to meet.

ONOTO WATANNA

XLIX

Oh, how good it was to enter New York once more! I remembered how ugly the city had looked to me that first time when I had come from Boston. Now even the rows of flat houses and dingy tall buildings seemed to take on a sturdy and friendly beauty.

Paul was walking up and down the station, and he came rushing up to me, as I came through the gates. He was pale, and even seemed to tremble, as he caught me by the arm and cried:

"When you did not come on that train, I was afraid you had changed your mind, and were not coming back to me. I've been waiting here all day, watching each train that arrived from Providence. Oh, sweetheart, I've been nearly crazy!"

I told him about the fire, and he seized hold of my hands, and examined them.

"Don't tell me you *hurt* yourself!" he cried. And when I reassured him, it was all I could do to keep him from hugging me right there in the station. All the way on the car he held my hand, and although he did not say anything at all to me, I knew just what was in his heart. He loved me, and nothing else in all the whole wide world mattered.

He had helped me out at the studio building, and now as I went up the old rickety stairs, I realized that this was *my home*!

It was a ramshackle, very old, neglected, rickety sort of place, and I do not know why they called it Paresis Row. The name did not sound ugly to me, somehow. I loved everything about the place, even the queer business carried on on the lower floors, and old Mary, the slatternly caretaker, who scolded the boys alternately and then did little kindnesses for them. I remember how once she kept a creditor away from poor Fisher, by waving her broom at him, till he fled in fear.

I laughed as we went by the door of that crazy old artist that the boys used to tease by dropping a piece of iron on the floor after holding it up high. They would wait a few minutes, and then he would come hobbling up the stairs. There would be three regular taps, and then he would put his head in and say:

"Gentlemen, methinks I heard a noise!"

On the first floor back a man taught singing, and he had gotten up a class of policemen. It seemed as if they sang forever the chorus of a song that went like this:

"Don't be afraid, don't be afraid, don't be a-f-rai-d!"

SEVERAL ARTISTS HAD COMMITTED SUICIDE in the building. I am not sure of the causes, and we never dwelt upon the reasons. There was nothing pretty about the place; it was cold and not even very clean; but—it was my *home*!

Paul opened the door of his studio. The place was all cleaned up and new paper on the walls. He showed me behind the screen a little gas stove, pots and pans hanging at the back of it, and dishes in a little closet. Then, taking me by the hand, he opened a door, and showed me a little room adjoining his studio. It seemed to me lovely. It was prepared in soft gray, and the curtains of yellow cheesecloth gave an appearance of sunlight to it. There were several pieces of new furniture in the room, and a little mission dresser. Paul opened the drawers, and rather shyly showed me some sheets, pillow slips and towels, which he said he had purchased for me, and added:

"I hope they are all right. I don't know much about such things."

I knew then that Paul intended the room to be for me. He had only the one studio room before.

"Well, little mouse," he said, "are you afraid to live with a poor beggar, or do you love me enough to take the chance?"

Thoughts were rushing through my mind. Memories of conversations and stories among the artists, on the marriage question, by some considered unnecessary and somehow with Paul it seemed right and natural, and the primitive woman in me answered: "Why not? Others have lived with the man they loved without marriage. Why should not I?" He was waiting for me to speak, and I put my hands up on his shoulders, and said:

"Oh, yes, Paul, I will come to you! I will!"

A little later, I said:

"Now I must go over to my old room and have my trunk and some other things I left there brought over, and I must tell Mrs. Whitehouse, the landlady, as she expects me back to-day."

"Well, don't be long," said Paul. "I'm afraid you will slip through my arms just as I have found you."

Mrs. Whitehouse, the landlady, met me at the door. I told her I was going to move over to Fourteenth Street, to Paresis Row. She threw up her hands and exclaimed:

"Lands sakes! That is no place for a girl to live, and I have no use for them artists. They are a half-crazy lot, and never have a cent to bless themselves with. If I were a young and pretty girl like you, Miss Ascough, I would not waste my time on the likes of them. Now there's been a fine-looking gent calling for you the last two days, and I told him you'd be back to-day. He's a real swell, and if you'd take my advice, you'd get right next to him."

Even as she spoke the front doorbell rang. She opened the door, and there was Reggie! I was standing at the bottom of the stairs, but when I saw him, I fled into the parlor. He came after me, with his arms outstretched. I found myself staring across at him, as if I were looking at a stranger.

"Marion," he cried, "I've come to bring you home."

I backed away from him.

"No, no, Reggie, I don't want you to touch me," I said. "Go away! I tell you go away!"

"You don't understand," said Reggie. "I've come to take you home. You've won out. I'm going to *marry* you!"

He looked as if he were conferring a kingdom on me.

"Listen to me, Reggie," I said. "I can never, never be your wife now."

"Why not? What have you done?" His old anger and suspicion were mounting. He was looking at me lovingly, yet furiously.

"I've done nothing—nothing—but I cannot be your wife."

"If you mean because of Boston—I've forgiven everything. I fought it all out in Montreal and I made up my mind that I had to have you. So I'm going to *marry* you, darling. You don't seem to understand."

Further and further away I had backed from him, but now he was right before me. I looked up at Reggie, but a vision arose between us— Paul Bonnat's face. Paul who was waiting for me, who had offered to share his all with me, and somehow it seemed to me more immoral to marry Reggie than to live with the man I loved.

"Reggie Bertie," I said, "it's you who don't understand. I can never be your wife because—because—" Oh, it was very hard to drive that look of love and longing from Reggie's face. Once I had loved him, and although he had hurt me so cruelly in the past, in that moment I longed to spare him the pain that was to be his now.

"Well? What is it, Marion? What have you done?"

"Reggie, it's this: I no longer love you!" I said.

There was silence, and then he said with an uneasy laugh:

"You don't mean that. You are angry with me. I'll soon make you love me again as you did once, Marion. You'll do it when you are my wife."

"No—no—I never will," I said steadily, "because—because—there's another reason, Reggie. There's some one else, some one who loves me, and whom I *adore!*"

I hope I may never see a man look like Reggie did then. He had turned gray, even to his lips. He just stared at me, and I think the truth of what I had said slowly sank in upon him. He drew back.

"I hope you'll be happy!" he said, and I replied:

"Oh, and I hope you will be, too."

I followed him to the door and he kept on staring at me with that dazed and incredulous look upon his face. Then he went out and I closed the door forever on Reggie Bertie.

THE EXPRESSMAN HAD JUST PUT my trunk in the studio. I opened the door of the little room that Paul had fixed up for me.

"Are you afraid, darling?" he asked. "Are you going to regret giving yourself to a poor devil like me?"

I answered him as steadily as my voice would let me, for I was trembling.

"I am yours as long as you love me, Paul."

I had started to remove my hat.

"Not yet, darling," said Paul, and he took me by the arm and guided me toward the door. "First we have to go to the 'Little Church Around the Corner.'"

THE END

A Note About the Author

Winnifred Eaton, (1875–1954) better known by her penname, Onoto Watanna was a Canadian author and screenwriter of Chinese-British ancestry. First published at the age of fourteen, Watanna worked a variety of jobs, each utilizing her talent for writing. She worked for newspapers while she wrote her novels, becoming known for her romantic fiction and short stories. Later, Watanna became involved in the world of theater and film. She wrote screenplays in New York, and founded the Little Theatre Movement, which aimed to produced artistic content independent of commercial standards. After her death in 1954, the Reeve Theater in Alberta, Canada was built in her honor.

A Note from the Publisher

Spanning many genres, from non-fiction essays to literature classics to children's books and lyric poetry, Mint Edition books showcase the master works of our time in a modern new package. The text is freshly typeset, is clean and easy to read, and features a new note about the author in each volume. Many books also include exclusive new introductory material. Every book boasts a striking new cover, which makes it as appropriate for collecting as it is for gift giving. Mint Edition books are only printed when a reader orders them, so natural resources are not wasted. We're proud that our books are never manufactured in excess and exist only in the exact quantity they need to be read and enjoyed.

bookfinity™

Discover more of your favorite classics with Bookfinity™.

- Track your reading with custom book lists.
- Get great book recommendations for your personalized Reader Type.
- Add reviews for your favorite books.
- AND MUCH MORE!

Visit **bookfinity.com** and take the fun Reader Type quiz to get started.

Enjoy our classic and modern companion pairings!

Classic & Modern

Printed in the USA
CPSIA information can be obtained
at www.ICGtesting.com
JSHW082336140824
68134JS00020B/1712

9 781513 271569